Deep in
CHAOS

CHAOS KINGS
MOTORCYCLE CLUB

LINNY LAWLESS

AMAZON BEST SELLING AUTHOR

DEEP IN CHAOS

Copyright 2019 by Linda Lawson

All rights reserved.

Cover Models: Garrett and Daria
Photographer: Lindee Robinson Photography
Cover Design: Charli Childs, Cosmic Letterz Cover Design
Editing and Proofreading: Mitzi Carroll and Marisa Nichols
Interior Design by Clara Stone of Reader Central
Personal Assistants: Mikki Thomas and Kristin Youngblood

To Simon, AKA Mr. Googles

PLAYLIST

CHAOS KINGS
MOTORCYCLE CLUB

Someone Like You / Adele
Hello / Adele
Send My Love (To Your New Lover) / Adele
When We Were Young / Adele
Water Under the Bridge / Adele
Make it Rain / Ed Sheeran
Don't / Ed Sheeran
Shape of You / Ed Sheeran
Perfect / Ed Sheeran

PROLOGUE

CHAOS KINGS
MOTORCYCLE CLUB

Tanya sat at the end of the black leather couch with her knees drawn up to her chest. As she listened to the sound of Matthew packing clothes in a duffel bag, she realized the piece of furniture she was perched on belonged to him too. Her eyes were swollen, and her nose was stuffy from all the crying she'd done in the past hour.

After coming home from work, she'd been greeted by the sounds of muffled grunts and moans coming from the bedroom. She closed the front door and heard a sigh that sounded decidedly female. She froze, her eyes boring into the door of the closed bedroom.

"Matthew?"

Her feet moved her toward the bedroom door. She heard another moan. Definitely female. She wrapped her hand around the doorknob and pressed her cheek against the door to better listen. Anxiety rose up inside her. She felt compelled to open that door, despite being afraid to see what lay behind it—like witnessing a car crash and being unable to turn away.

There was no turning back now. She turned the doorknob, opening the door to the nightmare her brain refused to comprehend for a moment. Matthew lay on his back—in *their* bed—sweating, moaning, his hips bucking, sucking the nipple of a plump breast. His hand squeezed the other breast of the curvy blonde woman it belonged to as she leaned over his body, riding him.

Fucking Matthew. Tanya's boyfriend.

The blonde opened her eyes, sat up suddenly, and gasped. Mathew opened his eyes when her nipple slipped from his mouth. Tanya stood motionless inside the door, unable to look away, not making a single sound.

Matthew came into the living room, his stuffed duffel bag slung over his shoulder.

"I didn't expect you home for another two hours, Tanya…"

"Oh, I'm sorry I got off work early and ruined your fuck fest in *our* bed." Tanya threw a black leather pillow at him.

"Apology accepted. I'm leaving now, and I'll stay over at Lou's house for a few weeks. I'll make arrangements to get my things moved out of the apartment."

"Some of these things are mine too." Tanya squeezed her eyes shut.

Matthew walked out the door, shutting it behind him, leaving her alone—betrayed. The tears freely flowed, spilling on the expensive leather couch.

SKULLY
CHAOS KINGS
MOTORCYCLE CLUB

I t was a hot, sticky night. My sweaty T-shirt clung to me as I sat in a shithole bar. I finished my third glass of whiskey and asked the skinny blonde bartender for another. I crushed out my smoke in the black, plastic ashtray, exhaling the last drag. A good buzz would kick in after the fourth glass. I kept my head down low, pushing my cap and craning the brim, scanning the bar. I was always alert. I had to watch my back; I was being hunted.

The Hell Hounds MC were after me now. If they found me, they'd kill me. But I had it coming. I was lucky that their Road Captain, Ratchet, didn't kill me that night. He was a big motherfucker too—he nearly crushed my fuckin' windpipe. It was Tanya who got him off me. Tanya—my sweet cheeks.

The second I saw Tanya, my heart slammed against my chest. I got Sam out of the Steel Cage and back to Tanya's apartment. Sid told me he was selling her back to Ratchet but didn't plan on giving her back to him. Instead, he made a fucked-up deal with those Russians. Now, thanks to the Russians, Sid was laid up in a body cast at Stayford Hospital with the prognosis of never walking again. He would have been better off getting a beat down from his dear ole dad, Knuck, the president of the Hell Hounds.

I was lucky the Chaos Kings didn't hand me back over to the Hounds that night. Chaos didn't give a shit about me. But I guess they weren't as fucked up as the Hounds. They knew I was a dead man anyway. So, after that night, I took off on my old shovelhead. It was a good bike. Went fast enough. But the next day I sold it to an old friend down south of the county line. Then I bought an '04 Super Glide. Flat black with a king/queen seat and the deal maker—two grinning skulls on both sides of the gas tank.

I was also paid up for a month at the shithole Del-Alton Motel, not too far from my buddy's bike shop. The room smelled like mold, which probably came from the shaggy seventies style, puke green carpet. The bed creaked on busted springs, but it was a place to sleep and out of the cross hairs of the

Hounds. I didn't want to leave the state. I grew up here.

I took off my Hound cut the night I left the Chaos clubhouse. I took it out into the woods behind the Motel, found a dirt clearing, dowsed it with lighter fluid, and torched it. The smell of burning leather and lighter fluid rose up into the night sky. I didn't want to be a Hell Hound anymore. I had seen too much. Done too much. All of it was bad—nothing good.

It's been a few weeks now. All I wanted to do was just get a good buzz. It sucked being alone. I lit another smoke, finishing off the fourth glass. I paid up my tab with the skinny blonde. She told me I shouldn't leave so quickly—she wanted to take a ride on my scoot when she got off in a few hours. I winked at her but told her maybe next time; I'd probably be back next week. She pouted, placing her hand on her jutting hip, and watched as I headed out the front door.

As I walked out, I recognized the two bikers as they swung their legs off their bikes. Hammer and Muddy—Hell Hounds. I lowered my chin and zipped up my hoodie, betting that the cap hiding my face and hoodie covering my ink would be enough to disguise me. Besides, it was dark out, and they wouldn't recognize my Super Glide. But then I inadvertently gave myself away, walking with the slight limp I'd been trying to make as part of my natural gait all my life.

"MotherFUCKER!" Hammer recognized the limp. I was only a yard away from my bike. Next two heartbeats, I swung my leg over my bike, started it up, twisted the throttle and burned rubber, leaving Hammer and Muddy with a mouth full of gravel dust. I opened the throttle wide open and rode balls to the wall a few miles down the main road. I pulled into the back of a gas station, pulled my lid out of my worn-out leather saddlebag, put the shades on and high tailed it back to my motel, watching my mirrors and listening for other sounds of pipes close by. I knew the sound of every Hound's bike—thankfully, none of them were Hammer's or Muddy's.

TANYA

CHAOS KINGS
MOTORCYCLE CLUB

I walked out of the salon after working ten hours on my feet again. Second time this week. I was exhausted. My calves and lower back ached. The tips and a full day of hair appointments was the payoff. I wasn't complaining. I needed every dollar I could earn. Matthew moved out six months ago. He took most of the furniture, like the expensive leather couch and loveseat set, which then left me with the rent, and I couldn't afford it by myself. I had to move into a smaller, more affordable one-bedroom apartment about ten miles away. Plus, the Chaos Kings didn't want me living there anymore because of what happened with Sam and the Hell Hounds. The Hounds knew where I lived, and Ratchet and all the brothers wanted me to be safe. Especially Magnet. We were childhood friends. We grew up together and from the same high school.

I didn't know where Skully went after that night. I kept telling myself I didn't care. Why should I? He was a Hell Hound. God only knew the things he'd done. And my blood was boiling when he showed up at my apartment with Sam. I was so scared but relieved that Sam was safe. He was standing right behind her when I opened my apartment door. Tall, dark hair. Not as broad as Ratchet but built all the same. Calling me sweet cheeks was *not* a good way to introduce himself to me, though—especially wearing a Hounds cut.

Even though I kept my distance from him, I couldn't let Ratchet smash Skully's throat in at the clubhouse. Skully *did* get Sam back to him and to Chaos. And he took off after Ratchet beat the shit out of Sid and the Hell Hounds left the clubhouse that night.

Sam was now Ratchet's ol' lady. Safe. Loved.

Ten p.m. and I dragged my feet up the flight of steps to my second-floor apartment. I walked down the hall to apartment 206, fumbling with my keys to find the one that fits in the door. Clumsy me dropped them. I knelt down, swiping them up and exhaling. As I rose, a hand cupped over my mouth, and my back was pressed up against a hard chest. I moaned, faint and muffled.

"Shh. It's Skully, Tanya. I'm not going to hurt you, okay? Will you nod for me?" Just a whisper next to my cheek. I nodded. His hand smelled like cigarettes.

"I'll take my hand away as long as you don't scream, okay?" I nodded again. "I'm coming in with you."

His hand came off my mouth, and I didn't scream. I found the key that fit the hole in the door-knob, unlocked it, and walked in. He followed behind and shut the door. I ran to the kitchen and pulled out the butcher knife from a drawer. I spun back around and pointed it at Skully, my eyes wide with fear.

He raised his hands up. "Whoa. I'm not gonna hurt you. I *can't* hurt you. Not in my condition, anyway."

That's when I took a good look at him. His lip was bleeding, and his left eye was a bit swollen. Only one arm was raised, the other wrapped over his chest.

I lowered the knife and placed it back on the kitchen counter behind me. "What the fuck happened to you?"

He walked over to my couch. I noticed the slight limp he had, wondering if it was just the way he walked, or if it was from a past injury. He dropped to the couch, slouching down to get comfortable. His head fell back against the couch pillows. He wasn't wearing his Hound cut—just a dark gray hoodie.

"Hammer and Muddy got me. Roughed me up a bit. Got away though." He closed his eyes.

I walked toward him, around the couch. "Why did you come here? You really scared the fuck out of me, you know that, Skully?"

"Okay, okay, Sweet Cheeks—"

"Don't call me that!"

His head came up from the pillows. "I wanted to make sure you were okay. I lost them, but I didn't want to take any chances."

"How did you know I even lived here?"

The side of his mouth lifted. His mouth was... sensual. "I know you moved out of the other apartment and into this one. I've been keeping watch over you."

His eyes squinted, wincing at the pain under the hand he had wrapped around his ribcage. I stood above him, hands on my waist. What the hell was I going to do with him?

"Did they break something there?"

He looked down and winced again. "Yeah. No. Maybe?" He leaned back into the couch. "I promise I won't do anything stupid. I just wanted to make sure you were okay. Don't want the Hounds to get to you..." His eyes closed as he mumbled to me. Then he began to snore.

I sighed. "Dammit..." I exhaled a breath. Kneeling, I grabbed his left boot and unzipped the side, pulling it off before repeating the process on his right. I gathered both his ankles and swung them up on the couch. Why? Hell if I knew. He didn't wake up. I locked my door and went to my bedroom to catch some much-needed sleep of my own.

SKULLY

CHAOS KINGS
MOTORCYCLE CLUB

"Wake up, Skully."

My head hurt. My mouth was dry. I opened my eyes. Sweet Cheeks was standing there above me. She was in a pink soft-looking robe, one hand on her hip, the other holding a coffee cup. Her brown hair was up in a messy bun. I blinked a few times to clear my vision. I sat up and swung my legs off the couch.

"If you want some coffee, go and get it yourself. This isn't a bed and breakfast." Her eyes were cold, her mouth tight.

I got up off the couch. I remember now why I was in her apartment. I walked up to the living room window, pulling the curtain just a bit to peer down.

"Where's your bike?"

"Parked it several blocks away. Traded the shovelhead for a Dyna."

I turned around from the window to look at her again. I had to admit; she was a hot looking chick. Those eyes, that auburn hair, her high cheekbones, and that pouty little mouth. I looked away. Had to. I went back to the couch to put my boots on. "You took 'em off?"

"Yes, I did. You passed out. Snoring away."

"Sorry about the snoring. Thanks for letting me crash here last night." I had my boots on. I stood up, putting me right in her personal space, only five inches away. We were so close, I could smell her hair —that flowery stuff they put in expensive shampoos.

She stepped back from me then, giving us distance. "I'll go now, Sweet Cheeks," I mumbled, staring at her mouth.

Her brows knotted together. "Don't call me that. Dammit!"

I chuckled. I liked how mad she got when I called her that.

"Well, you can't go looking like that, Skully. Sit down. You should clean up a bit. And how are you going to ride if your ribs are all busted up?" She left me, walking into her bathroom before coming back with a bottle of peroxide and a washcloth.

Opening the bottle and pouring some on the cloth, she brought it to my lip.

"Fuck!" My head snapped back.

"Crybaby." She pressed the cloth onto my lip again, but gentler this time. Then she pressed it up above my swollen eye.

"Oh, tough Hell Hound. Can't take a little pain?"

I reached up and wrapped my hand over hers. "I'm not a Hound. Not anymore, Tanya."

She was silent then, looking up at me. Her eyes turned soft. "If they find you, they will kill you, Skully."

I pulled her hand away from my swollen eye before turning away to walk to her door. "Yeah, I know. And my goal is to stay alive." I unlocked her door and turned back to her. "Lock up when I leave, sweet cheeks."

"Dammit, Skully!"

I shut it before she could charge at me.

My bike was right where I left it, five blocks away from Tanya's apartment. My rib was killing me. Hurt like bloody hell. I swung my leg over my Dyna and high tailed it back to my shitty motel room.

I was relieved Hammer and Muddy lost me after I got a good ass beating the night before. I didn't go back to that shithole bar they'd seen me. Unfortunately for me, though, they found me again at a fuckin' gas station. Had to fill up the tank on the bike and pay cash to the old man at the counter inside. When I heard the pipes, it was too late. I stepped outside and ran to my bike, but they got me. Roughed me up right there by the gas pumps. Muddy got my face. Once I was down, Hammer kicked his boot into my side. Hurt like hell. From far away came the sound of police sirens, and they were off me, taking off on their bikes. I got up off the oil-stained asphalt, climbed on mine, and burned rubber before the cops pulled in.

But if they found out where Tanya lived, I wouldn't ever forgive myself. It would have been my fault if she ever got hurt—or worse. A rock dropped down to the pit of my stomach every time I pictured those motherfuckers touching her. I'd seen how they hurt other women. And all those times I didn't stop them. I would always carry that guilt around my neck like a fuckin' albatross. But how could I protect her? The gimp ex-Hound who just betrayed his club. She would be much safer with the Chaos Kings MC. I knew this, but I had to see her again.

TANYA

CHAOS KINGS
MOTORCYCLE CLUB

I was in a rare mood. All because of him. That smartass, Skully. He had the *nerve* to scare the hell out of me the night before. And coming into my apartment uninvited! I hated to admit to myself that morning that I did sleep well. He was roughed up a bit by the Hounds, but knowing he was sleeping on the couch outside my bedroom made me feel safe for the first time since Matthew left.

I was finished with my last customer for the day, an elderly woman named Patricia. She was a regular client of mine, in her seventies, who told me of her growing up in the 1950s and how things were so different then than they are now. She had white hair, and I would set it in curlers for a permanent. She reminded me of my grandmother.

Patricia noticed my furrowed brows and how I'd rarely smiled since the beginning of her appoint-

20

ment. I was in my own world all day. I told her not to worry; I was just tired and needed a vacation. She patted my hands with her soft ones when she gave me her tip.

Honey, the store owner and manager, wanted to close early after Patricia left. It was a slow night, and there were no more appointments.

"Anything going on tonight at your motorcycle gang party house, Tanya?" Honey was a sweet, energetic woman in her late thirties with red hair and fair skin.

"The Chaos Kings are not a gang, Honey. They're a club. A tribe. There is a big difference."

"Okay, sorry 'bout that. So, is the MC having a party tonight?"

"Yeah. Why? You want to come along this time?"

She was closing the cash register and doing all the accounting stuff only she knew how to do. She stopped counting the cash in her hand, then turned to me and grinned with a wink. "Sure, would love to!"

She recently had a bad break up with a longtime boyfriend and wasn't having any luck with the online dating thing. She was getting tired of all the blind dates her friends were setting her up with. I figured she wanted to go out and be social again. Meet some of my friends in the Chaos Coven.

The clubhouse was jumping early tonight. Music was blaring, cue balls knocking against each other on the pool tables, clouds of weed or cigarette smoke drifted our way as I walked in with Honey. Of course, Magnet was the first one to notice me and grabbed me around the waist, picking me up off the ground with his warm hug.

"Hey, baby!" I really needed that hug from my childhood friend.

Hey, sweetie. Still love those hugs."

He put me down, and his eyes went straight to Honey. "Introductions, Tanya."

I rolled my eyes as he reached down and took Honey's hand in his. "Honey, this is Magnet. Magnet, Honey."

Her eyes were wide when she looked up at him. He had that effect on women—that's why he was called Magnet, as in "Chick Magnet." I waved my hand in front of her. "Honey, I'll grab us both a beer. Hang out with Magnet, if you like. He can show you around."

"Oh, I sure will, babe." Magnet winked at me, then started up a conversation with her.

I left them, shaking my head, and walked up to the bar to see my favorite couple, Ratchet and Sam. They were sitting close together, kissing. Sam was so small next to Ratchet's huge frame. He was a quiet one—had a low, gruff voice—but he had a huge heart.

Sam broke their kiss when she saw me coming toward her. She jumped off her barstool and wrapped her arms around me. "Tanya, baby!"

I squeezed her tightly back. She was the bravest woman I knew. She was abused and treated as property to the Hell Hounds MC, but she'd dared to make a better life for herself and escaped that hell—landing right on Ratchet. You could see how much he loved her; they looked like two teenagers finding love for the first time.

I remember that feeling. That first time with love. I felt it with Matthew.

My phone vibrated in my back pocket as I released Sam. I pulled it out. Matthew's name appeared on my screen with a new message.

Matthew: "I'll stop by your apartment this week to get the last of my things."

I did have a few boxes of his things. I packed it all up for him and moved it with me to my new apartment. Not sure why. I should have just thrown it all away. I didn't think he missed it anyway. It was only a few books and photo albums.

Chickenshit couldn't talk to me on the phone. I pushed the call button next to his name. It rang twice, and he answered.

"What, Tanya?"

"Are you bringing your new blonde girlfriend with you to my apartment?"

"Her name is Melissa. And she's not my girlfriend."

"You fucked her in *our* bed, and you don't even classify her as your girlfriend? Why not? She looked like she had nice childbearing hips."

It came out of my mouth. The most painful part of this break-up with him.

"Tanya. That's not the reason we're over. You know what those reasons are."

I couldn't listen to his voice one second longer and hung up on him. I squeezed my eyes shut. When I opened them, Sam was looking at me, and I realized she'd heard all of it.

Sam tilted her head. Ratchet came up and stood behind her, placing his big hands on her shoulders. "Don't let him bring you down, Tanya," Sam said. "He doesn't deserve someone like you."

I shoved the phone back in my pocket, looking down at my car keys. "I wish I could believe that."

"Sam is right. He's a low-life. He's not worth one more minute of your time." Ratchet grumbled. He didn't say much, but when he did, it meant something, and I appreciated it.

I wiped the last tear I was going to shed for Matthew "Okay. I need a beer. And I need to get one for Honey, my boss. She's over there getting verbally seduced by Magnet." I pointed in their direction. Honey was now batting her eyes at Magnet, standing close.

Three beers later, and I was a little buzzed and exhausted. Magnet promised he would give Honey a ride home on his bike and she was ecstatic. I left the clubhouse alone and drove the back roads home since I drank three beers and worried I would blow past the legal limit if I got pulled over. My little crappy Ford Escort was acting like a grumpy bitch lately. I needed to get her checked out soon; she'd stalled on me a few times lately. I figured it had to be a bad fuel pump.

And she decided to do it to me again only five

miles from my apartment. I kept pressing on the gas, but she sputtered. I pulled off the two-lane road. It was dark out, and I was surrounded by trees that blocked out the moonlight. I turned the ignition off.

"Dammit! Why now?" I yelled and leaned my head back, shutting my eyes.

It was hot and steamy out. The air was so thick with humidity that your clothes stuck to you. I felt it the moment I shut the damn car off. I popped the hood under the dashboard, and when I climbed out of the vehicle, that sticky air hit me. I broke out in a sweat instantly. I pulled the hood up, not knowing what the hell I was going to be checking for anyway. I knew nothing about cars.

I heard the pipes and saw the one headlight of a motorcycle just fifty yards away, coming toward me on the dark road. I froze. I was alone. My phone was on the passenger seat in my car. The bike pulled up behind my car, the headlight aimed at me. I couldn't make out who the rider was, and I didn't recognize the sound of the pipes. They didn't sound like any of the Chaos brothers.

This was bad. I snapped out of it and moved toward my car door to get my phone. But the biker was there before me. It was a Hell Hound. He was tall with long reddish hair tied back underneath a black lid with stickers all over it. He had a long beard, messy and wind-blown.

"Let's talk, Chaos cunt!" He was quick, grabbing a fistful of my hair. He slammed me against my car door. The air was knocked out of me as I braced my arms in front of me to cushion the impact.

It hurt, and I was frightened for my life. I was in shock and couldn't move. He wrapped his hands around my waist and flipped me around. This time, he slammed my back against the door. He reached up with one hand and wrenched both my wrists above me. His other hand was on the outside of my blouse and grabbed my breast.

"Where is that gimp motherfucker hiding out, cunt?" It was Rusty. The Hell Hound who hurt Sam. He was looking for Skully. His breath smelled like cigarettes and liquor.

"Get the *fuck* off me, you piece of shit!" I screamed at him. I spit in his face. His head snapped back when it landed between his eyes, on the bridge of his nose.

"I like it when you bitches fight back..." The hand on my breast dove down in the front of my jeans. I kicked and screamed.

"No one is gonna hear you out here. What's so

special about your pussy? That gimp Skully seems to like it."

White lightning pain shot through me as he thrust two fingers roughly up inside me. I screamed. I kicked him. Then he was wrenched out of me and out of my jeans. I heard a man's roar, and I felt the humid air against me again.

It was Skully. He had Rusty by the shoulders as he pulled him off me. He swung him around and threw him to the asphalt in the middle of the road. Rusty landed hard on his back. Skully was on top of him, punching him over and over. Blood spewed from Rusty's nose, his mouth.

Skully stopped. He leaned back, breathing hard and fast. He looked back down at Rusty's bloody face.

"You ever fuckin' touch her again, you're dead." He inhaled mucus from his throat and spit it in Rusty's face.

He leaped off him, but Rusty didn't move. I reached out to him, collided into his chest, and held him tight as I started sobbing.

His arms wrapped around me. He smelled of sweat and blood. He was so warm, breathing fast.

"I'm here, Tanya. I got you." He held me, letting me scream and sob into his chest.

I grabbed my purse and helmet from the backseat of the car and locked it up. I always had a lid with me in the car, just in case.

I held on to Skully tight as he drove me back on his bike to the clubhouse at way above the speed limit. I was okay with that. I was still in shock and wanted to get far away from Rusty, whom we left there in the road, bleeding.

We pulled into the gravel lot of the clubhouse. Most of Chaos was still there, music blaring from inside and filtering outside. Skully stopped and planted his feet down on the gravel, yards away from the other parked bikes. The only thing the club members could see was his headlight. He turned his head toward me.

"You okay to go to them by yourself? Don't think they'd like it too much if they see me with you."

"Rusty was looking for you. All of them are after you. You're not safe alone. Pull into the lot. I got this," I said low against his ear.

"If you say so, Sweet Cheeks." I wasn't so mad this time to hear him call me that.

We walked together from the lot into the club-house, all members staring with daggers in their eyes at Skully. We weren't surprised, of course. Ratchet and Magnet headed right for him as we entered the clubhouse. Honey followed behind Magnet. I put both my hands up to them. "I want him here with me. He just saved me from being raped by that nasty disgusting Hell Hound, Rusty."

Sam had been standing behind Ratchet, but when she'd heard what I'd said, she quickly maneuvered around him to stand in front of me and grasp both my arms. "Are you okay, Tanya? Did he hurt you?"

"Oh my god, Tanya! Are you okay?" Honey was right there next to Sam, wide-eyed and shocked.

"I'm okay. He hurt me a little. But it could have been worse if Skully wasn't there..." I turned my head to see him standing right behind me. Close. The cut on his lip was scabbed over, and he tilted his chin up, his lips in a straight line, eyes on Ratchet before falling on Magnet.

Ratchet stared back at him. "Where's your car, Tanya?"

"It stalled on me again... On Leeland Road."

"Again?" Magnet's eyes left Skully to focus on me.

"Yeah. I think it's something with my fuel pump. Filter? Something like that."

Ratchet rubbed his face with both hands and grumbled. "I'll get it towed in the morning for you. And get it fixed. If you can't afford it, the brothers will help. Don't go driving the car again if you think it's running funny."

"Okay...Thanks, Ratchet. I learned my lesson. Now, I need to be alone for a moment—and Skully is staying. He's not leaving. The Hounds are after him. He's not safe alone." I walked into one of the bedrooms down the hall.

Skully followed and shut the door behind him. "I'm sorry, Tanya. If I'd only been there a minute sooner, he wouldn't have gotten to you."

"Not your fault. Glad you were there." My voice was shaky.

My body started to shake, and for the second time that night, I cried as Skully wrapped his arms around me.

"Shh...I got you...You're okay now. You're safe." He whispered down into my hair as I sobbed. I gripped the front of his hoodie jacket with both hands. He was tall. The top of my head touched his chin, sprouting a week-old dark growth of a beard.

I pressed my cheek against his chest. His heart pounded hard and fast. I hiccupped and sobbed. His deep voice rumbled in his chest against my ear, and it soothed me. I went silent, just to listen to that heartbeat.

"Your hair smells good. You use expensive shampoo, don't you?" he mumbled in my hair. I started to giggle.

"Well, duh. I *am* a salon specialist, Skully." I looked up at him until our eyes met. We both stood there frozen.

He could have kissed me at that very moment. I wanted to know what his sensual mouth would feel like against my lips. But he lifted his eyes from me and looked up at the ceiling. He stepped back but kept his hands braced on my arms.

"You going to be okay? I better scoot on out. Your Chaos brothers don't like me one bit."

"Well, you're safer here with Chaos than alone. But I can't stop you from leaving."

"Stay close to them, Sweet Cheeks." The side of his sensual mouth rose in a smirk, winking at me. And then he left.

SKULLY

CHAOS KINGS
MOTORCYCLE CLUB

The Chaos Kings let me be as I left their clubhouse. My blood boiled as I squeezed the throttle, and my pipes thundered wide open back to my shitty motel. Ever since that morning I left Tanya's apartment, I kept a distance but kept watch over her. I was hiding out like a fucking coward. I knew Rusty and the Hounds would find some way to get to me. I'm sure they had tons of intel from that chick, Mandi. She knew most of the Chaos brothers, the women, and ole ladies. It was my fault Tanya got hurt. I came up on her car and Rusty's bike. Then I heard her scream. When I saw Rusty touching her, I was enraged. It happened so fast, and I don't remember the details; I just remember pulling him off her and pounding his face in.

I couldn't get Tanya out of my mind. She was such a spitfire. A protective she-lion over Sam that night I got her out of the Steel Cage. I had my share of chicks. Some in high school and of course, I banged some of the Hell Hound club whores. Always made sure I kept my decent-sized cock wrapped every single time too. But there was something about Tanya. She had those high cheekbones and cute lips. I jacked off every night, thinking only of her.

I should have left town. I was done with being a fucking Hell Hound. I was done even before I helped Sam get away that night. I did my fair share of shit for the club—money, drugs, anything they needed. But now I had a reason to get out. And the moment Tanya cried in my arms, I knew. I also realized that night that Chaos was different from the Hounds. They weren't a diamond club. But they didn't beat and humiliate their women like the Hounds. I witnessed it time and time again and never did anything about it. What could I do? I knew what it felt like to be humiliated, beaten down. So, I wanted to change my tune. And I knew what I needed to do first before I could move on.

It was noon the next day and hot as fuck out. No clouds, only humidity. I walked into the darkness of the Steel Cage. It was cool inside. I bought a burner phone and called Knuck, the President of the Hell Hounds MC. Told him I'd come in, but that I wanted a meet—just the two of us. The heavy beat of the music was already pounding through the club as I walked in. Some of the girls were into their first round of dances either on the stage or the three cages set in each corner.

Some of the Hounds were there, sitting with Knuck at the same booth those Russians sat at the day they made a deal with Sid to buy Sam. I walked, showing as much confidence as I could, trying to improvise my slight limp so that it was in rhythm to my stride. I was scared shitless though. Knuck told the other Hounds to leave the fuckin' table as I stepped into the light from the overhead ceiling lamps.

Knuck leaned back in the booth, exhaling a drag off a cigar. "You got balls, Skully."

"I'm out, Knuck. Done. If that means you put a bullet in my head, there's nothing I can do about it."

"And you're a dumb shit for not leaving town, brother. You know I can't let you hang around my town after that fucked up stunt you pulled getting that club whore out and fucking up Sid's plans."

"I was going to leave. But I just can't."

Knuck sucked in and blew another drag of his cigar. He tapped the ashes into the red glass ashtray. He chuckled, shaking his head. "Well, I gotta admit. You helped me out. I'd never make that kind of deal my dipshit son made with those Russians." And he handed his son over to them.

"So, what do we do now?" I wasn't backing down. I wasn't leaving.

"You've been my best moneymaker, Skully. You don't gotta leave. Sit down. Let's talk."

"Rusty got to her last night. I could have killed him. So, before I do sit, I need your word that Tanya is safe from this minute on."

TANYA

CHAOS KINGS
MOTORCYCLE CLUB

The next morning, Ratchet towed my car to a local mom and pop auto shop not too far from my apartment. I was right. It *was* the fuel pump, and it had to be replaced. My car would be in the shop for a few days. Honey gave me the day off after what had happened the night before. I was shaken up. Rusty violated me. I woke up with bruises on my wrists and one on my back from when he slammed me up against my car. I felt disgusting. I took a hot shower to wash off the filth I felt covered my body.

The next day, Honey picked me up for a full day of work at the salon. She had gone home with Magnet after the clubhouse party. I looked at her as she drove. She had an unmistakable glow to her face and a smile that stretched from ear to ear. "How you feeling, sweetie? I hope you got some rest yesterday."

"I'm feeling better. Thanks, Honey. So, was Magnet a gentleman the other night? You tell me if not. He's like a brother to me, and I *will* kick his ass if he wasn't."

She turned to me, and her face went a shade deeper than before. "Yes. He was a total gentleman. And totally naughty too."

I just rolled my eyes at her. "Oh, god. Don't want to know. I've heard way too many stories of his naughty side." I loved Magnet like a brother, but his sexual conquests were just not something I wanted to hear about.

Honey sighed. "Okay, sweetie. Enough about me. I was so afraid for you the other night. Are you going to report the assault to the police?"

I never thought of reporting it to the police. I was still shaken up inside. I kept thinking about Skully. How he held me and comforted me before he left. How badly I wanted him to kiss me. How I shouldn't think about him at all.

After a long day, Honey dropped me off at my apartment. My car wouldn't be ready until tomorrow. I went to my fridge and poured myself a glass of

Moscato. Three knocks on my apartment door. I looked through the peephole. Matthew. Handsome as always, wearing a gray suit, his tie loose.

"What, Matthew?" I didn't want to see him.

"Just stopping by to get the rest of those boxes of mine, Tanya."

I opened the door. His eyes met mine. Matthew was tall and physically fit, due to his strong dedication to eating right and working out, and he had light brown hair and brown colored eyes to match.

He came in and walked past me, looking around at my small one-bedroom apartment. "Looks nice, Tanya."

I walked past him into my bedroom to get the box I packed for him when I moved.

I carried it back and handed it to him. "Here you go. Your photos and other things."

He took it from me. "Take care of yourself, Tanya."

My blood pressure rose, and my voice came out a little too loud. "What the fuck, Matthew? Don't say things you don't mean!"

He leaned down and dropped the box. "Just trying to keep this civil. You've been hanging around your biker friends way too long to know *how* to be."

"You really mean the *biker trash* I hang out with,

Matthew. Sorry my tribe doesn't meet the standards of your civilized, materialistic, shallow world!"

"Bye, Tanya. Good luck." He picked up the box and left.

I was so angry. I needed to get out and blow off some steam. It was Saturday night—perfect for a girl's night and the best excuse to get totally trashed.

I finished my glass of wine and called Honey. She was game. I called some of my girls in our Chaos Coven to join me at the CrowBar. Honey picked me up, and once I got there, I planted myself at a table that sat six and Greaser served us both a round of cocktails and Buttery Nipple Shots.

Within half an hour, my coven began to show up: Madge, Rusty's ol' lady, and my brave girl-friend, Sam. She had some anxiety coming to the CrowBar, but Ratchet dropped her off on his bike and walked in with her. He gave Madge and me a hug, then gave Sam a steamy kiss and swatted her ass before he left. Sam's co-worker friend, Kat, showed up too. She was nice, albeit a bit shy. My other coven wenches, Toni and Andrea, showed up. They were salon specialists who I worked with in the past, and they loved hanging out with my Chaos brothers.

As the night went on, more people showed up at the bar for Saturday night craziness and Sunday morning hangovers. My table kept Greaser and his waitress busy with the cocktails and shooters coming.

The girls clapped and whooped and hollered as I downed another shooter, slamming the shot glass back on the table and wiping my lips with my forearm. "Fuck being civilized! It's all about being primitive!" Greaser came back to our table, placing another round of drinks on our table. I wasn't even finished with the one I was currently attacking.

"Ladies, this round is from the dude at the bar." I turned in the direction of Greaser's nod. It was Skully. He looked right at me with a smirk and nodded. My stomach did a flip. He was alone at the bar, under a Tiffany lamp hanging from above him. He wore a black Harley Davidson T-shirt that hugged his biceps and his chest. The whole coven turned to look at him, too.

"That was nice of him, Tanya. Maybe you should go over and thank him?" Sam was the first to say something, as all the other girls' mouths hung half-open.

I didn't see him walk in. I guess I was just too

busy working on getting my drunk on. "Okay, Sam. You're right." I rose from my chair and walked over to him, feeling a little light-headed.

He watched me come toward him. "Thanks for the drinks, Skully. I thought you would have left town by now."

His dark eyes were so intense. They wandered from my hair to my lips and stopped. "Change of heart, Sweet Cheeks. I'm not going anywhere. Good to see you."

My tongue was tied for a second, dumb struck by his eyes and his sensual mouth. The alcohol was doing its job of making my body flush, my face blushing.

"And how are you going to pull that off? The Hounds are after you."

"I talked to the Prez. We came to an agreement. And a promise. You're safe. That motherfucker Rusty or any of them won't mess with you ever again."

I looked down. I could still feel Rusty's hands on me. Inside me. Skully's finger reached over and lifted my chin to look at him again. "I'm so sorry I didn't get there in time, Tanya. I could have killed Rusty. And I will next time if he's even in the same *vicinity* as you."

I had to look away. His deep voice and his eyes were drawing me in to step even closer to him. "Well, thanks for the other night. And thanks for the round of drinks you sent to my coven wenches." I turned to walk away.

His warm hand grasped my wrist. "Wait." I turned back to him. "And I want to thank you for letting me crash at your apartment the other night." He was off his barstool. He took a step closer to me. I had to lean my head back to look at him. I noticed scruffy beard was growing out. "I didn't expect to see you here tonight. I'm glad I did."

My stomach did another flip. My breathing sped up a bit. He was standing too close. I felt the wetness between my thighs. I stepped back. I had to. "I have to get back to my table and continue to get loaded."

"Wait." He still held on to my wrist. "I need a favor."

"You're running out of favors, Skully."

"I want a meet with your Chaos brothers. Ratchet, his Prez. Can you help me make that happen?"

"Why? What are you up to now? Did you like Ratchet smashing your windpipe that night at the clubhouse? Because that's what might happen again."

"No. I want to square things up with Chaos." It showed in his eyes that he was serious—determined.

I was still, staring into his eyes. What could it hurt? Skully did save Sam. I know both she and Ratchet appreciated it.

"Okay, Skully. One more favor. I'll make some calls. Get you that meet with Chaos. Give me your phone; I'll add my number." He handed me his phone from the bar, and I added myself into his contacts. "There you go. I'll text you the time and place to meet." I handed his phone back. The side of his mouth lifted as he saw my name lit up on the screen.

He smiled as I walked away. "Have fun, sweet cheeks." I was angry at myself this time...because I realized I was getting used to him calling me that.

SKULLY

CHAOS KINGS
MOTORCYCLE CLUB

I had to hand it to Tanya. She talked to her brothers that same night and texted me in the morning. I was to meet with Ratchet, along with the President, Rocky, Gunner, and Magnet at the Chaos Clubhouse that night at nine. I parked my bike in their lot ten minutes early. Their bikes were already there, parked alongside each other.

I walked into the clubhouse, feeling like I was crashing their party again. Gunner and Magnet were at the pool tables. Magnet was taking his shot but rose when he saw me. Ratchet and his President had just slammed some shot glasses on the bar, and their eyes shifted to me too.

Ratchet rose off his bar stool. "You're both brave and stupid, Hound."

I gave him a nod. "Yeah. I'm both. But I'm not a Hound. I'm out."

"So, why the fuck you following our sister Tanya around? Why are you even still in this county?"

Magnet was on me in an instant. He was my height, standing only inches from me. His jaw clenched. It ticked, and his hands were balled into fists at his sides. "Tanya is like a sister to me, motherfucker. You're no good for her, Hound. Stay the fuck away from her."

I glared right back at him. Stood my ground. "I just told your brother I'm not a Hound anymore. And Tanya can decide if she wants me to stay the fuck away or not."

"Motherfucker!" Magnet shoved me. Hard. I stumbled back a few steps. My balance was off, and I almost landed on my ass, but I stabilized myself at the last second.

The Prez was off his stool, holding Magnet back. "Come on, Magnet. This is all Ratchet. Not you."

Ratchet didn't move. I wasn't sure where Gunner was, but I just realized that maybe I wouldn't be walking out of here in one piece. "I had a talk with Knuck. The Prez. I planned on leaving town, but I wanted to square things up with you and your brothers."

Ratchet was smiling. "So, say what you need to say. You got one minute. I'm counting."

"I'm good with Knuck and the Hounds. I'm out. I want to get that money back to you. The bag of cash you gave to Sid. So, Knuck gave me a choice. I get the money back to you, but the Hounds get their go at me. Or Knuck keeps all of it, and I'm out, untouched. And I'll have to fend for myself against Chaos."

Ratchet jutted his chin out, scratching his beard. His eyes stared off, contemplating. I was fucked if he really wanted that cash back.

"Don't give a fuck about that money. I just give a fuck about Sam. She's mine now. My ol' lady. That Hound can keep it all." He grumbled and turned to sit himself back on his stool and poured another shot of whiskey. "I owe you anyway. For saving her." He downed his shot and slammed the glass on the bar.

"So, we're good?"

"Yeah. We're good."

I did walk out of the Chaos clubhouse that night. And in one piece.

I met with Knuck again at the Steel Cage the next day. "Ratchet doesn't want the money back. It's all yours, Knuck. So, I'm out."

He looked hungover. He finished off the last of his whiskey as we sat in the same booth alone together again. "That so?" His voice sounded rough.

"You gave me two choices. And I chose."

"You think you can go legit just like that, huh? I've known you a while now. You never wanted to turn before. The Hell Hounds took you in. You belong here. You moved up the ranks, started out as a low-life prospect and took all the shit the Hounds fed you. What are you gonna do now? All you know is fuckin' pussy and making money for the club."

"I'll either get locked up again or get dead if I keep wearing the Hound patch. I'm done, Prez."

He tapped a chunk of his burnt cherry in the glass ashtray and he chuckled. "All about pussy, isn't it? I saw what you did to Rusty's face. You didn't like what he did to that chick you got a hard-on for. I can't keep Rusty on a leash. He's still pissed as all hell about what you did to get Sid fucked up by the Russians. He was foaming at the mouth to have that VP patch. Now it ain't happenin'. So, you're on your own with him."

"I did what I had to do before I became a Hound. And I'll keep doin' alone. Nothing new for me, Knuck." I walked out of the Steel Cage. In one piece.

TANYA

CHAOS KINGS
MOTORCYCLE CLUB

link. Something hard hit my bedroom window.

Clink. Another one. I walked over to the window. My heart skipped a beat. Standing at the street corner just below my window was Skully. I didn't see his bike, just him under the streetlight, turning his head left and right. He looked up, his arm prepared to throw another object again at my window.

What the hell is he doing? And why the hell this late at night? I slid the window up. "Don't you *dare* throw one more thing at my window, Skully!"

I got his attention right as he was mid-throw. He stopped, lowered his arm, and smiled as he ran a hand through his dark hair. "Okay, okay. Just wanted to get *your* attention and no one else's."

"What the hell are you doing here? Where's your bike?"

"I parked it a few blocks away. Didn't want anyone to see it parked in front of your place. I'm here cause I wanna take you out. Go out for coffee. Grab lunch—go on a date. Aw, hell, Tanya ..."

I worked hard at keeping the smile off my face. "Well, what is it. then? Coffee? Lunch? Or a date, dammit?"

"A date! Will you go out on a date with me?"

I couldn't help but smile then. I had to admit, it was kind of sweet in a way. Even though my shields were up, I couldn't deny how brave and wild he was, which made my stomach do one of those somersaults again. "No. Not a date. Let's do coffee first, okay?"

"Okay, sure. A coffee date it is. I'll be back in the morning to pick you up." He beamed up at me, grinning from ear to ear under the streetlight.

As he walked away, down the street, my smile faded. *It's not a date! It's just coffee!* And besides, what harm is there in just having coffee with an ex-member of the Hell Hounds MC, an enemy of my tribe, the Chaos Kings MC?

I waited outside in the parking lot of my apartment, with my lid and my purse strapped across me. It was another humid, hot morning, and it wouldn't even be noon for the next three hours. I heard Skully's pipes a few blocks away. He rode up to the stop sign and turned his bike, heading toward me. He wore a simple black tank top that hugged his body, and my breath hitched at the sight of his inked shoulders and forearms. He stopped alongside me and planted his boots down on the asphalt, twisting the throttle a few times, making his pipes rumble with a wide grin on his face.

He pulled his shades down his nose, and his eyes roamed down my body, from my hot pink tank top to my tight skinny jeans and black boots. He whistled. "Hot damn... You sure are pretty in pink, Sweet Cheeks." My nipples instantly hardened at the sound of his voice. I hoped my bra showed off my cleavage and not my perked-up nipples.

I strapped on my lid, climbed on his bike behind him and placed my booted heels on the passenger foot pegs and put my hands on his hips. "I wear pink like a boss, Skully. Now, take me for a ride."

"You sure as hell do, baby." Skully pulled in the clutch, tapped his booted toe down into first gear, twisted the throttle and rode me out to the café.

I really needed to ride. I missed it. While Matthew didn't ride—he hated bikes—Magnet would take me out sometimes. Riding with Skully was different though. The vibrations felt good on my ass and thighs, making me wet between them. He smelled of some manly body spray mingled with his own sweat, which acted as an aphrodisiac to my senses.

We took a seat at one of the bistro tables outside of the café. Skully went inside and brought me back an iced vanilla latte. He had a big cup of hot coffee. He pulled out a smoke and lit it. "This is not a date, Skully."

"It's Owen."

"Owen?"

"Yeah. That's my name."

I liked it. "So, Owen, why does everyone call you Skully?"

He blew out a drag of his smoke, leaned down and tapped his right shin. "Dirt bike accident. I was a stupid teenager. Spiral fracture. The tibia and fibula. Not stupid anymore. Just a little reckless sometimes."

"But how does your leg get you the name of Skully?"

"Fractured my skull too. Healed back on its own. Skully is what I got stuck with along with that limp

I'm sure you noticed." I had noticed his slight limp. But it didn't detract from my intense attraction to him. He made it his own. He walked that limp like a boss.

"Enough about me. I took you out for a ride to get to know you, Sweet Cheeks."

"Stop. You want to get to know me? Call me by my name."

His lip lifted in a smirk. "Okay. Tanya. Did you grow up here in Stayford?"

"Yes. Grew up, went to high school. I'm the only child. My parents retired and live in Florida. I visit on the holidays."

"How long you been with Chaos?"

"I grew up with Magnet. He's like a brother to me. He lived across the street in my neighborhood. He joined the Chaos Kings several years back, and of course, I followed along. I'm not someone's ol' lady though." I stopped. Few moments of silence.

"Why not?" His head tilted slightly, his eyes staring into on mine.

"I was in a long-term relationship. But not with a Chaos King." At that very moment, Matthew appeared, walking right up to our table. Walking with him was that blonde I found him fucking in our bed months ago. She held onto his bicep.

"Hi, Tanya." He actually smiled at me. Skully looked up at Matthew and dragged his shades down his nose to get a better look.

"Hi, Matthew." I nodded to Skully. "Meet my friend, Skully—I mean, Owen. Owen, this is Matthew and his friend...Melissa, was it?" I looked right at her. That tramp had the fucking nerve to smile at me and at Skully too.

Skully was out of his chair and raised his open hand to Matthew. He just looked at his hand and nodded. "Owen."

Skully lowered his hand and pulled his shades back up to cover his eyes. But he didn't sit back down.

"Another one of your biker gang buddies, Tanya?" Skully took a step toward Matthew. I was right. He was a few inches taller. Blonde tramp girl stepped back, pulling on Matthew's arm.

"Yeah, I *am* one of her biker gang buddies. Get used to it, motherfucker." Skully growled low, his jaw set.

"Come on, honey. I need my mocha latte." Melissa pulled Matthew back. They walked away and into the café.

Skully watched them until the glass door closed

behind them. He sat back down and turned to me. "Was *that* the long-term relationship?"

"Yes. We broke up six months ago..." My cold vanilla latte didn't taste so good anymore. "Can we go now?"

He reached across the table; his warm hand covered mine. "Sure, Tanya. Come on, let's go. I wanna ride you..." He smiled and winked. "On my scoot."

SKULLY

CHAOS KINGS
MOTORCYCLE CLUB

I felt Tanya relax behind me as I took her down backroads away from the coffee shop. Her hold on me around my waist loosened a bit. She leaned with me into the curves, the hot air pushing against both of us.

Instead of seeing the fire in Tanya's eyes, I saw... embarrassment? Hurt? I figured the dude "Matthew" was an ex-boyfriend. I knew little about Tanya, but I planned on getting to know more. But that douchebag fucked the whole coffee date up.

I pulled into her apartment parking lot. I planted my boots to steady the bike, and she climbed off. She unstrapped her helmet, not saying a word. She kept fumbling with the strap to her lid.

"You owe me, Sweet Cheeks."

"I don't owe you shit, Skully!"

"Whoa, Tanya. Just coffee. I still want us to have

that coffee date." Her fingers froze from fumbling with the strap under her chin. I reached up to loosen it for her.

"Sure. Okay. I'll make you a cup," she mumbled. Her breath on my knuckles made me all butterfingers, and now I was fumbling with her strap. I finally got it loose enough for her. She took it off as I worked on mine. I kicked my stand out and climbed off the bike, hanging my lid on the handlebar and followed her up the stairs to her apartment.

I sank into her comfy couch and bounced a couple of times. "I slept pretty well on this the other night."

Pretty in pink was making that pot of coffee in her kitchen. "Well, glad I could make that happen for ya, Skully." It was a mumble, but I heard it.

I got up off the couch and walked over to her in the kitchen. Her brows were furrowed. I guessed her mind was still thinking about the ex-douchebag boyfriend. "That douchebag doesn't look like your type."

She looked up from pouring water into the coffee maker. "How the fuck do you know what my type is?" She came at me and stopped only a few inches away, her jaw jutting out, eyes lit with anger.

I raised my hands. "Whoa, it's a compliment. I don't know much about you. Yet. But I just don't see it. You deserve someone who puts you first. That guy Matthew thinks he comes first. Before you. Before that chick hanging on his arm. And he seemed to have a problem with your Chaos brothers. They're just dirty biker bastards to him." She lowered her eyes. I moved toward her and lifted her chin and our eyes locked. "You deserve a man who puts you first, Tanya."

She stepped back and was up against the refrigerator. I moved in and touched her lips with mine. Soft. She moaned, and then her lips pressed harder against mine. She wrapped her arms around my neck. Her fingers combed into my hair, and she pulled. My tongue invaded her lips and wrestled against hers. My dick sprung to life and pressed up against my zipper.

She moaned again. I pulled away and dropped to my knees in front of her. She looked down at me, her eyes glossed over. I clutched both cheeks of her plump ass. I buried my face in between her thighs and inhaled her scent. Her hands were still tangled in my hair. I leaned back, unbuttoning and unzipping her jeans. I yanked them down, along with her lacey hot pink panties, and smashed my mouth up against her sweet pussy. My tongue darted out and right up the middle of her slit. Her head fell back, and she cried out. She tasted so sweet.

"You're fucking delicious, Tanya. I knew you would be."

"Kiss me, Owen," she pleaded. I stood up and leaned into her for another taste of her mouth. My dick was hard as a fuckin' rock, to the point of pain. She reached down and rubbed her palm down my length. Now it was my turn to moan.

Not sure why, but she suddenly stopped kissing me. Stopped touching me. She stepped back. "What the hell are we doing?"

I had to steady myself. Get my pounding heart back to a normal pace. "I'm not apologizing for what just happened. You want it as much as I do. That's why I stuck around. I can't stop thinking about you."

She folded her arms, and that heat in her eyes disappeared. "Well, you're going to have to stop thinking about me, Skully. This *will not* go anywhere. It shouldn't have gotten this far anyway."

I turned away and headed toward the door. "You can say that again, Sweet Cheeks."

TANYA

CHAOS KINGS
MOTORCYCLE CLUB

I opened my door. "Wait, Owen!" He stopped and turned around to look at me. His brows furrowed. "I didn't mean that. Dammit. I don't know."

He walked back to me. "What do you want, Tanya? Tell me."

"I want to start over."

He reached up and trailed his finger down my cheek. His mouth lifted into a smirk. "Okay. We can do that."

My eyes betrayed me as tears sprung and ran down my cheeks, onto his finger. "He ripped my heart out. I can't get it ripped out again. I'm afraid to feel anything again."

"Your heart's still there, Tanya. I can feel it. I'm afraid too. Maybe I *should* have left town. After I settled things with Knuck and the Hounds. I'm good with your Chaos brothers too. Not sure about Magnet, though. He cares about you."

"Yes, he does. He's like a brother to me. After Matthew ended it, Magnet was there for me. All of Chaos was there for me."

His finger left my chin, and he shoved both hands into his jean pockets. "How about this. I'll step back. I need to get my act together anyway. Find me a good *legit* job. Start over."

No more tears sprung. My lips lifted in a smile. "Sounds like a plan, Skully."

"Take care, Sweet Cheeks. I had a great time with you today." He smiled and turned back toward the stairs. I heard his pipes rumble to life as he started his bike and rode away.

I sat in Ratchet's kitchen with Sam. I called her a few days later because I needed a friend to talk to. Other than Magnet, of course. Sam brewed us both some coffee, and I told her about Skully. The ride, the coffee shop, his kiss. I left out that he licked my pussy.

"I never had a chance to thank him myself,

Tanya. For his help to get me away from Sid and those Russians."

"He's out. He's not a Hell Hound anymore. He made his peace with them and with Chaos too."

"And you're attracted to each other."

She was smiling when I lifted my eyes from my coffee cup to her. "Shit...Yes...Is it *that* noticeable?"

"Yes. It is."

I started shaking my head. "What the hell do I do about it?"

"You can't help being attracted to someone, Tanya. I couldn't help it when I first met Ratchet. Love is chaotic."

"Whoa! Who said anything about love?"

"Well, not just love; feelings too. Feelings can be chaotic too. It just never makes sense, I guess."

"He even asked me what I wanted. With Matthew, it was always what *he* wanted. It was never about me."

"Skully is not Matthew."

"You can say that again!" We both busted out laughing.

"So, what did you tell him?"

"That we should start over."

"Well, you just answered your own question, sweetie."

The next day my car was ready, so Magnet gave me a lift to the auto shop. He picked me up on his custom Softail. It was neon yellow, with a stretched-out springer front end and high bars. He only had a p-pad on the back fender that I had my ass on so many times before. The back pegs were up high, so my knees were up, in the breeze.

With the roar of his pipes, there was no way he could talk to me during the ride. But once we got to the auto shop and off his bike, he let me have it.

"So, that Hound still around? Is he bothering you, Tanya?"

"He's not bothering me. We went out for a ride on his bike and had some coffee. That's it."

"What the fuck? I told that motherfucker to stay away from you!"

"Cut it out, Magnet. I know he made peace with the Hounds and he's good with Chaos too. He hasn't done anything to hurt me. Besides, it's up to me who I ride with, have coffee with, who I fuck. Not you."

Magnet raked his hand through his short light brown hair. He looked down, shaking his head. "Yeah, that's all up to you. Just don't want him coming around the clubhouse."

"Magnet, he never had a beef with you. Matter of fact, he helped Ratchet. He helped Sam. Do you know what would've happened if he didn't save her? She'd be shipped off somewhere by Russian sex traffickers. And what do you think would have happened to Ratchet? He would have signed his own death warrant. He would have gone after the Hell Hounds and anyone who even had a Russian accent! And he'd be dead by now."

"Damnit, Tanya. You're like a sister to me. I just don't want to see you crushed again like you were with that douchebag, Matthew."-

I laughed. "That's what Skully called him too."

"Well, we both can agree on that." His mouth lifted into a smile. He reached out and wrapped me in his arms. "Okay, sis. You're a big girl. You know how to take care of yourself. And I know for sure you call the shots with Skully."

"Thanks, Magnet," I mumbled into his chest and closed my eyes, soaking in the brotherly love.

TANYA

CHAOS KINGS
MOTORCYCLE CLUB

T he only good thing that came out of it was Noah. If I didn't have him, I would have had to suffer this alone.

"Who was it, Tanya?" He sat with me in on the couch in my parent's basement. His arm was around my shoulders, his brows drawn together.

"It doesn't matter now, Noah," I said and hunched over, wrapping my arms around my stomach. The pain of an intense cramp shot through me.

Noah held me as I rode through the pain. He didn't know what else to do. I was just glad he was there, and that he kept this a secret between us. No one could find out. No one in school. Not even my parents. He lived across the street and went to the same schools, all the way up to high school. And it was our senior year.

He drove me to the clinic. After it was done, he drove me home. Both my parents were at work, so it was just Noah and me.

SKULLY
CHAOS KINGS
MOTORCYCLE CLUB

I stayed out of Tanya's way for a few weeks. I thought it best to give her some space. I didn't want to smother her. Especially after I tasted her lips and her sweet pussy. My dick was so hard, it hurt. I had to jack off when I left her apartment that day. I had a history of banging chicks, before and during my days with the Hounds. Didn't even remember their names. And yeah, I jacked off a lot too just for maintenance. But there was something about Tanya, and of course, I wanted to fuck her. A lot. When I rode up to her that day, she was standing there with that hot pink tank top and tight-ass jeans. Her neck had a sheen of sweat, and her hair was damp from standing in the hot sun, waiting for me.

I couldn't stop thinking about her. The look in her eyes when I left her apartment. Pain? Sadness? Fear? Maybe all three. But I needed to see her again.

I sent her a text, asking if she'd meet me for a drink—not coffee this time. She replied yes, and she'd meet me again at the CrowBar. I had the sudden urge to jump on the shitty bed with the busted spring in my motel room. But I kept my cool and steadied my racing heart.

I pulled in and parked my bike in the lot at the CrowBar. I was about fifteen minutes early. I climbed off, unfastening my lid, surveying the lot. Plenty of trucks, cars and other bikes, but I didn't see Tanya's car. I went inside and sat at a small table for two near the pool tables. I ordered whiskey, neat, from the blonde bartender and lit a smoke. The first taste of whiskey felt good going down, mixed with the taste of my half-smoked cigarette. I waited and looked around. A couple of bikers were playing pool, all dressed up in their leather do-rags and shiny new leather vests. A few others were bellied up to the bar, or they sat at some tables, laughing and drinking.

Ten minutes later and into my second drink, Tanya entered and walked toward me. I admired her high cheekbones—a feature that helped make her cute as ever. She wore tight-ass jeans and a flowy black blouse. As she walked toward me, her hips swayed slightly, but not intentionally. It was part of her walk. She was a bit taller, wearing some black wedge sandals, with her hot pink toenails peeking out from the straps.

She tilted her head when she sat across from me in the empty chair I saved for her. "Were you here long?"

I swallowed and found my voice. "Not long. I'm just on my second drink. What would you like?" I went to the bar to get her requested rum and coke and a third drink for me, then I brought them back to our table. She thanked me and took her first sip.

"How have you been?" I asked as my opening line. Not great, but I wanted to begin again where I left off—getting to know her.

"Busy at work." She put her glass down. "Two weeks? Takes you that long to ask me out again?"

"I thought it best you have your space. I didn't want to smother you with the look of me for a while." I wanted to be honest and up-front with her. "I also needed to figure out what to do next, since I don't wear the diamond patch anymore. So, I got a job."

Her mouth lifted into a smile. "Well, that's a start." She tipped her glass at me. "Congrats, Skully."

"Yeah. A legit job too. My buddy that owns that bike shop, Hardcore Cycles, next county over. He sold me that Dyna. He needs help in the garage—

just basic mechanic stuff. I know my way around a bike, so I took the job."

Silence. I reached across the table and covered her soft little hand with the hot pink nail polish. The skull and crossbones tattooed on the top of my hand caught her attention. "This is some nice ink, Skully." She traced it with her index finger. Her light touch sent goose bumps down my back. My cock jumped and slammed up against my zipper.

She looked up into my eyes. I made sure my jaw didn't drop. "Yeah. It hurt like a motherfucker. But I guess it should if it's there forever. That way, you don't forget." She pulled her small hand away. "Did I say something wrong?"

She reached for her drink again. "No. It's okay."

I leaned in and ran my calloused finger down her soft cheek. "Didn't mean to say something to make you look so sad, Tanya."

She leaned into my hand. "It's okay, Skully. I'm just cranky and tired tonight. Let's talk and share a few drinks, okay?"

"Sure thing, Sweet Cheeks . Sure."

Moments later, we both turned toward the entrance of the CrowBar, as Rusty stumbled in. Tanya's eyes were round as saucers, and her mouth dropped open. She reached into her purse and pulled out her phone. Her fingers moved over the screen as she started to text, those hot pink fingernails clicking away.

"Who are you texting?"

Her brows knotted, concentrating on her texting. "Magnet. Ratchet." She tossed her phone on the table and stood up.

I grabbed her wrist. "Where you going?"

"I'm going to do what that piece of shit did to me."

I was off my chair. "Wait. Sit here for a few more minutes. He didn't recognize my bike out front. He's shit-faced. Probably high on meth. Wait until your Chaos brothers get here. That's why you texted them just now, right?"

She sat. "Okay. I'll wait a few minutes longer."

We waited and watched Rusty. I was right. He was shit-faced and harassing the blonde bartender. Ten minutes had passed when I heard two sets of pipes thundering into the lot outside. It had to be Magnet and Ratchet.

Tanya was off her chair again. "Okay, let's do this."

I followed right behind her as we approached Rusty. He was hunkered down in his stool, grumbling and chuckling. Magnet came first through the front door, with Ratchet behind him.

Tanya stood right behind Rusty. "Hi, Rusty. Remember me?"

Rusty heard her soft voice and slowly turned around on his stool, grinning. He didn't recognize her. Tanya's hand shot out, right between his legs, and grabbed a handful of both balls and dick. Rusty's eyes bulged out of his skull, and his face turned red in the blink of an eye. He yelped like a dog and froze.

"You don't remember me, Rusty? Well, I remember you. I remember your putrid breath and disgusting hand down my pants a few weeks ago. Is that how you treat women? How does it feel when a woman grabs you back?"

Magnet and Ratchet were standing behind me by then, and they both chuckled. I couldn't help but laugh along with them. The sight of Tanya gripping Rusty's man parts was a good image to remember for a long time.

Rusty held his breath as he struggled to speak. "Skully is not a Hound anymore. He's protected. By Chaos."

She let him go, and he leaned over, gulping air back to his lungs. She turned from him and moved to stand behind me, resting her hand on my bicep.

I pushed Rusty back up to a sitting position on his stool, grabbed the front of his cut and growled, "Yeah, motherfucker. I had a chat with Knuck. I'm out. And I'm good with the Hounds. But I'm not good with you. And neither are the Chaos Kings. Stay the fuck away, Rusty. Stay far away." I let go, pushing him back up against the bar. "Now, pay your tab and get the fuck out of here."

TANYA

CHAOS KINGS
MOTORCYCLE CLUB

I climbed on Skully's bike behind him. I never rode in wedge heels before, so I made sure the soles were firmly planted on both foot pegs. I wrapped my arms around his waist. My hands pressed tight up against his T-shirt, feeling his muscled abs beneath it.

"Take me for a ride, Skully. I don't care where. Just ride," I purred against his ear above the loud rumbling of pipes. I inhaled beneath his earlobe. His scent made my stomach do one of those flips, and I was suddenly wet.

Skully kicked his heel down into first gear and rode us away from the CrowBar. I kept my arms wrapped around him and rested my cheek on his shoulder. The humid night air pushed against us. I shut my eyes and let him ride me wherever he wanted. It seemed that both Magnet and Ratchet's apprehension of Skully being around me eased a bit after I took care of Rusty. They were there for me like they always had been. And now they knew that I was safe with Skully.

He took me down heavily-forested back roads. I leaned with him as he took the sharp curves. He pulled into Mountain Lake County Park. It was late, and the park was secluded. He parked the bike next to a few picnic benches under huge oak trees.

"Don't get off. Stay right there." He pulled off his helmet, placing it on the ground, and climbed back on the bike, facing me.

We were tilted a bit, but the kickstand and his body kept us balanced. He leaned in and kissed me softly. His hands reached up for my helmet strap. He continued to kiss me, maneuvering his warm hands to unstrap my lid. I felt it lift off my head and land on the ground next to his.

He broke the soft kiss and leaned back. "I've never met a woman like you, Tanya. I can't stay away from you for so long. I need to see you. Just be around you."

We both still had our shades on, and it was a dark night. I couldn't see his eyes, but I wanted his lips again. I grabbed the back of his head, pulling him to me and crushing my lips against his. He drove his tongue into my mouth. I inhaled deeply, my tongue colliding and curled around his.

"Let me touch you..." he mumbled against my lips.

"Mm-hmm," I moaned back.

One of his hands reached up under my blouse and glided up my stomach to my rib cage. His other hand worked on unbuttoning and unzipping my jeans as he wrestled his tongue against mine. My bra cup was shoved down, and my nipple hardened instantly. They both ached as his finger and thumb twisted and tugged on it lightly. I cried out against his mouth as his other hand glided down into the front of my jeans. His finger slid along the outside of my wet pussy.

"Fuck, that feels good, Owen. Keep going, and don't stop." I breathed out.

"Yes, Tanya. Whatever you want." Then his warm finger penetrated deep inside me.

I cried out as my hips gyrated against his finger, gliding it in and out. I arched my back, so his thumb and finger kept teasing and tormenting my hardened nipple. Both my hands roamed down his muscled abs, and he tensed and tightened. I reached down further and rubbed his thick hard bulge.

He moaned. ", Tanya. I'm so fucking hard for you, it hurts."

"It doesn't have to hurt; I can make it stop. I'll ride you and make it all feel so much better." I surprised even myself for saying something so uninhibited.

It would have been impossible to ride his hard cock on the bike, leaning on a kickstand. So the next thing I knew, we were parked in front of his motel room. We climbed off his bike, hanging our lids and shades on his seat and handlebar. He took my hand and lead me a few feet away into his room.

He led me inside and closed the door. It looked like any other cheap motel room. The bed was made, and the furniture was very retro seventies style, there was even a shag carpet. I walked toward him; he stepped back. I noticed his slight limp, but it didn't impede his balance. He stopped when the back of his legs hit the bed. I pushed him, and he fell, landing on his back. I climbed on him and straddled his waist, caging him in.

My hips moved, rubbing down along his hardness. Our clothes were still on, but the friction made butterflies flutter in my belly. He shut his eyes and moaned, grabbing my hips.

"I'm going to take what I want. And you're going to give it to me."

His eyes opened suddenly. "Yes, Tanya. Take what you want from me."

I climbed off him and began to strip. He sat up, watching me peel off my top and bra. I wasn't trying to be slow and seductive. I kicked off my heels and shimmied out of my tight jeans. His speed in shedding his clothes matched mine. I was back on the bed, straddling him.

My pussy was soaking wet, and I was ready. And he was rock hard and ready too. I reached down between us, guided him to my opening. I lowered myself onto his cock as he slid up inside me, slowly. We cried out together when I was fully impaled on his engorged shaft. I froze, my head falling back. He felt so good filling me up, stretching me.

I took his hands and raised them above his head, pinning them down to the bed. I rode him, and his ass lifting off the bed and back down again, slowly at first, his rhythm matching mine. Then my hips picked up speed, and I fucked him, sliding up and down on his eager cock.

"I can't...hold back...I'll come inside you..." He

gritted his teeth, his voice strained. An orgasm exploded from within me, and my whole body jolted with spasms. My inner walls squeezed his cock, and I cried out.

"Cum inside me. Now!" I commanded. He growled as his rock-hard dick squirted hot cum against my cervix.

I released his hands and collapsed over him. My cheek rested on his hard chest, his heart pounding. My breasts crushed against him. A sheen of sweat covered our bodies, and the smell of sex permeated the motel room. I closed my eyes and steadied my breathing. His strong arms wrapped around me.

"It doesn't hurt anymore," he mumbled against my ear. It was the last thing I heard before we both fell asleep, holding each other.

SKULLY

CHAOS KINGS
MOTORCYCLE CLUB

I woke up in a hospital bed. The back of my skull throbbed with pain. The same throbbing pain pulsed down my right leg. My eyes opened. I looked around the room. Denise was there, sitting in a chair next to the bed. She was my social worker and custodian., a plump middle-aged woman, her short blonde hair cut in a bob.

Denise was dressed in a navy-blue suit, and she smiled at me. "Don't get up, Owen. Just relax." She was off the chair and stood beside the bed next to me.

"What happened? Where am I?"

"You had an accident on that dirt bike, Owen. You broke your right leg, and you have a slight fracture on the back of your skull." Her smile faded, and her eyes looked worried.

The pain throbbed in those exact places on my body again. I shut my eyes, hoping that it would block out the pain. The darkness behind my lids helped me remember what happened. It was summer. I was out with some of the neighborhood boys I hung out with. They lived in the same neighborhood as my foster parents...Tony, Jeff, and Randy. They pushed me around and sucker-punched me at school. But I dealt with it. I didn't care much when they bullied other boys—and even girls sometimes—because I just wanted to belong. If I hung with them, I thought they'd have my back.

We were hanging out by the electrical powerlines. Tony and Jeff had dirt bikes. I watched them on the rolling dirt hills along the high electrical poles. They took turns riding up and down the hills, and Randy was good at it too. They showed off to some of the other boys and girls who hung out with us. We'd smoke some weed, drink some cheap beer someone would steal from their parents' refrigerators. I wanted my chance to ride one of those dirt bikes, to prove that I could ride just as good as them.

"Okay, numbnuts, go ahead and try it. Don't cry like a pussy if you fall off the damn thing." Tony sneered at me. He pulled his bike up alongside me. It was a bright green Kawasaki, with bumpy treaded wheels for the sole purpose of dirt bike riding. He climbed off, handing me his helmet, as I took the handlebars from him. I climbed on, not knowing what the hell to do.

Tony's hands were on his hips as he chuckled. "Hold in the clutch, kick it into first gear. Let off the clutch and ease on the throttle...Dumbass!"

I did as he said, and I was moving. I shifted into second gear, riding along the rolling dusty hills along the powerlines. I picked up speed and shifted to third. I suddenly got a hard-on. I had already banged a few chicks in high school, so popping a boner riding a dirt bike made me realize that I loved riding on the two-wheeled machine.

The rush of adrenaline made me brave when I saw the rising of the next hill, and I twisted the throttle. But I gunned it too fast. The momentum lifted me off the seat. From then on, I remembered nothing, just darkness. It was like being asleep for a long time. And then I woke up there in a hospital bed.

"You'll be in that cast for a while, and the fracture on your skull needs to heal. Your foster parents can't afford the medical bills. You now belong to the state. And I'll be your guardian until you're eighteen, Owen."

TANYA

CHAOS KINGS
MOTORCYCLE CLUB

I woke up next to Owen with my arm draped over his hard chest. He was sleeping, giving me a chance to look at him. His dark brown hair was short and messy, pressed into the pillow. His chin sprouted a few days of unshaven beard. He had long dark eyelashes that any girl would kill to have. His breathing was steady. Then his eyes fluttered open, and he looked at me watching him.

The side of his mouth lifted in a smile. "How long have you been awake, Sweet Cheeks?"

I couldn't help but smile at that quirky nickname he gave me. "Not long; I just woke up too. You need to ride me back to my car at the CrowBar. I need to get home." I climbed over him and off the bed and started to get dressed.

He rose, leaning his head into his hand. I looked at his muscular bicep as he watched me put my clothes back on. "Do you have to get back so soon? Why don't we get some breakfast, or some coffee, maybe?" He was off the bed, and his cock was thick and hard like the night before. It took all the control I had not to push him back on the bed and ride him again.

"No, Skully. Maybe some other time."

"Was it something I did last night? I'm sorry, Tanya...I should've stopped and put a condom on."

I stepped back from him. "Are you clean? No STDs?" He shook his head. "Okay, then. Don't worry about it. I can't get pregnant."

"So, you're on the pill or something?"

"No! Goddammit! I can't get pregnant, Skully! I can't have children!" I barked.

His arms came around me then. He was so tall and his hard body so warm. I didn't want him to know about the defective part of me. I wondered why I even told him. I pulled away. "Just take me back to my car. Like, now."

It was careless and reckless to fuck Skully without a condom. But it happened. If I wanted him again, and I already knew I would, it was best to be honest and tell him about my infertility. Once it came out, I couldn't take it back.

We were both silent on the ride back to my car. I

climbed off his bike, unstrapping my lid. "Thanks for last night and the ride, Skully. And good luck with your new job."

"Can I see you again soon? And I don't mean just to fuck. Take you for another ride? You sure do make me *and* my bike look good with *you* on it." He smirked.

I couldn't help but smile back. "Sure, I'll go for another ride with you. Soon."

SKULLY

CHAOS KINGS
MOTORCYCLE CLUB

I t was my second week on the job at Hardcore
Cycles. I was getting the hang of it, just basic
maintenance, and oil changes on bikes. My
buddy and my new boss, Torque, who owned the
shop, was pretty laid back and trusted me.

I thought about Tanya and what she said about
not being able to have kids. I felt her pain, felt it
physically. How ironic that I grew up in foster homes
all my life because whoever my parents were, they
didn't want me. I didn't know what to say to her
when I dropped her off to get her car. She was silent
behind me the whole time as I wrapped my hand
underneath her soft, plump thigh. She responded
with a gentle squeeze with her inner thighs. But I
could tell she didn't feel like talking.

She took control that night in my motel room.
Every time the images came flooding back into my

mind, I'd get hard, and the front of my jeans felt tight, even when I worked at the bike shop. How sexy she looked and how soft she felt on my cock. Her luscious thighs straddling me. She took what she wanted—and she wanted me, just as much as I needed her. I needed to see her again. And soon.

My dick jumped when my phone lit up with her name and a text:

"CKMC is getting together for a charity ride. Do you want to ride along?"

It took me a few seconds to type a text back to her, my thumbs fast and clumsy on the screen.

"Sure. When? What time?"

"Sat, 11am."

I rolled into the lot of the Chaos Kings' clubhouse on my Dyna and planted my feet down on the asphalt. The lot and entrance to the clubhouse were packed with about a hundred bikes and double that in people. It was a warm morning already, and most of the women were in shorts and tank tops. Some of the men wore their jean or leather vests. It was way too fuckin' hot to layer up, and wearing the bare minimum was my plan.

I found Tanya instantly in the crowd. She wore a hot pink tank top, white shades, tight-ass jeans, and white boots. She looked so goddamn pretty in that pink...She saw me too and waved me over to her. I shifted back into first gear and rode toward her. I was very aware of all the Chaos Kings and other bikers, exhaled with relief knowing that I looked like everyone else, another biker wearing a gray tank top.

Tanya tilted her head slightly and smiled. "Thanks for coming along for the ride, Skully."

I shut the bike off, kicked the stand down and climbed off. "Thanks for the invite." I pulled out my smokes from the tool bag on my bars.

"You can take your lid and shades off and chill for a bit. We're still waiting on a few more people to join the ride. Come on. Let's go inside. I need to give out some hugs and say hello to my tribe."

I followed her into the clubhouse. I hadn't been there since I had the talk with the Chaos brothers. I spotted Ratchet with Sam at the bar, exactly where Tanya was leading me to. Both girls squealed and hugged each other. I looked at Ratchet and nodded. He nodded back, which was all I needed from him to know that we were good. I grabbed a stool behind Tanya as she talked with Sam a bit. I took a drag from my smoke, surveying the place.

Magnet walked up to the bar and stood right beside me, but he didn't turn to look at me. He asked the cute blonde behind the bar for a beer, and she handed him one. When she walked away, he still didn't look at me.

"You hurt her, I hurt you." He twisted the cap off his beer and took a long swig.

"I don't intend to." I didn't look at him either. Then he walked away.

By the time I was done with my smoke, the other group of people we were waiting on pulled into the lot. There were several road captains, including Gunner and Ratchet, who kept small groups together for the ride. Bikes were started back up, lids strapped on, shades down.

Tanya walked with me to my bike, strapping on her lid. "I'm glad you came, Skully."

"I'm glad too. I want you to ride with me, but I don't want to rub anyone in the club the wrong way. I'll get in last and ride in the back with one of the groups—if that's good with you."

"Sure. No one is going to get rubbed the wrong way. I invited you and Chaos is okay with it."

"Whatever you say, Sweet Cheeks," I replied and couldn't help but flash her a dorky grin.

The President and VP, Rocky and Spider, led

the first group out. We rode behind Ratchet and Sam. Tanya leaned back on my sissy bar. She relaxed and didn't say much. I could see her in my side mirror. The sun was shining on her face, her white shades making her look like a magazine cover model. She was a natural when it came to riding on the back of a motorcycle. Some people tensed up, but she didn't. We were both part of the thundering machine that vibrated between our legs.

We rode out west toward the Shenandoah Mountains. The smell of summer, green leaves, and grass surrounded our senses. And sometimes, even the stink of roadkill hit our noses. When you rode on a bike, you smelled everything. The groups made a few stops after a two-hour-long ride. Later in the afternoon, we rode back. Some riders went home or stopped at different bars, but most returned, kicking their stands back down at the clubhouse.

The lot was already full when I pulled in with Tanya. Loud music blared out from the clubhouse as we climbed off the bike. Handshakes, slaps on the back, and hugs were passed around, everyone ready to let loose. Tanya grabbed my hand, and my heart thumped hard in my chest. I followed her back into the clubhouse; we grabbed a few cold beers and stepped back outside.

"So, what's it like now, not wearing a diamond patch?" Tanya sipped from the bottle with her pretty pink lips.

Not belonging to a club, whether a diamond club or not, made me feel a bit lost. And alone. I took a long swallow of mine. "Weird. I wore that Hound patch for three years. "

"Is it scary too? I mean, making such a huge step out like that?"

"Yeah, pretty fuckin' scary. But I've been scared before. Many times."

She was smiling, but it faded. She looked away. "I'm sure you have. You sure don't show it though."

I took a step closer to her. She looked up at me. Her shades were still on. "You don't show it either, Tanya. I thought you were badass for grabbing Rusty's junk like that. I've never met a woman like you."

"Yeah, I'm one of a kind, huh? Maybe that's why I'm defective."

I reached and curled some of her pretty brown hair behind her ear. "Tanya, it's just the hand that was dealt to you. But you're not defective. Do you think I'm less of a man because of my limp?"

She exhaled, her breath caressing my wrist. "No. Not at all. I think your limp is part of you. It's sexy..."

I leaned in and kissed her like I did at the park the other night. Her tongue darted into my mouth. I pulled away, smiling down at her. "Thanks. Took me years to perfect that limp."

She smiled, but her mouth latched back onto mine. Her hands were in my hair. I pulled her in, pressing her up against my chest. I became hard quick. Then she moaned into my mouth.

"I know you want me, Tanya," I growled low against her lips.

"Yes, I do, Owen. I want you." She pulled away and took my hand, and I followed her back into the clubhouse. I didn't care if anyone watched us, my focus was on her sweet ass. I admired it as she led me down the hallway and into one of the rooms.

The moment I shut the door, Tanya was on me. She covered my mouth with her sweet, soft lips, and our tongues caressed and wrestled together. She jumped and wrapped her luscious thighs around my waist. I claimed her ass cheeks with my hands, spun around, and pressed her back against the door. My dick was so fucking hard, it hurt, just like it did before I was deep inside her the other night.

I shoved my hips right up against her center. "I need you, Tanya. Make the pain go away again."

She sighed as my lips placed soft kisses down her

cheek to her jawline. My tongue darted out and glided down the side of her neck. I licked, nipped, and sucked while carrying her to the bed. I gently placed her down on her back and slid down her body, unbuttoning and unzipping her jeans. I pulled her boots off, then her jeans. My hands nudged her thighs open, and I shoved my face right up against her delicious, hot pussy. She cried out as my tongue penetrated her wetness and caressed her swollen clit, gliding up and down, and back up again. My hands squeezed the soft flesh of her thighs. They opened wider, giving me the go-ahead to feast on her even more.

"Holy fuck!" she cried out as I tasted her orgasm on my tongue. Her fingers raked through my hair and pulled.

She pushed me away and sat up. "Get those jeans off, Owen. I want that nice hard cock of yours inside me right fuckin' now."

"It's all yours, baby." I couldn't get my jeans down around my ankles fast enough before I covered her with my body. I gripped my solid rock of a cock and drove myself all the way inside her. I grunted as I pumped into her hard, my hips moving, pounding her as hard and deep as she wanted.

"I can't get enough of you, Tanya. I'm hungry

and thirsty for you every fuckin' minute of the day." I growled as I looked at her pretty face and fucked her the way she liked it. Her lips parted, and her eyes were hooded, moaning and panting along with the rhythm of my hips. I had to shut my eyes. If I kept watching her, I would explode.

"Don't close your eyes, Owen. Look at me." I did as she said, and I couldn't hold back any longer. I roared and exploded as my cum shot inside her hot, silky center. I collapsed on top of her. We were both out of breath, covered in sweat.

Her arms wrapped around me. "What are we doing?" she whispered.

"I don't know. But I sure do like it," I mumbled, nestling my face against her neck.

TANYA

CHAOS KINGS
MOTORCYCLE CLUB

The charity ride was a success, and the Chaos Kings raised close to three thousand dollars for the local county animal shelters in the area. That giddiness I felt riding with Skully was exhilarating. The combination of riding with my tribe and Skully nestled between my thighs made my pulse race. I had a splendid view of his broad, V-shaped back and toned shoulders, making my mouth water and leaving me soaking wet down below.

I felt the release of endorphins tingling all through my body when I orgasmed on his tongue. And when he came inside me, it was a rush of pure erotic heat that rushed through us both. We laid there for a few minutes together, his face nestled against my neck.

But the loud music and sounds of laughter came

from outside the door, and it woke us both up, making us realize again where we were. We got dressed and walked back out into the main area of the clubhouse, and to the sounds of whistles and hoots and hollers from most of the men. I rolled my eyes, but Skully, of course, had a wide shit-eating grin on his face.

I was giving a perm to one of my clients, but staring off into space, re-hashing the entire day in my head. "Did you have a nice weekend, Tanya?" My client, Betty, brought me back to the present.

"Huh? Yeah, Betty. It was nice. Why?"

"You've got that dreamy look, and you're smiling too. So, don't stop. It's looks good on you."

I guess I hadn't realized it, but everyone else had. "Thanks, Betty," I replied to her as she beamed a smile at me.

Before Skully left the clubhouse, he asked me what I was doing later in the week. He wanted to take me out on another date. I told him I had Wednesday off, and that I'd drive to the cycle shop to meet him. "It's a date!" He grinned and kissed me before he rode away.

I took my time Wednesday morning and slept in, then I sipped on my coffee and by ten a.m. I primped in front of the mirror longer than I usually did. I made sure to wear some tight jeans that made my ass look really good, plus a hot pink leopard print blouse, and finished my outfit off with wedge sandals. I applied a little extra lip gloss, tussled my hair a bit, and put on my white shades. I left my apartment and drove to Hardcore Cycles.

Clouds were dark and heavy in the sky, ready to dump buckets of rain. The humid air enveloped me as I walked to my car. It was a bummer because we wouldn't get a ride on Skully's bike that day and would have to drive somewhere instead. Lightning and thunder cracked as I pulled up into the parking lot of the bike shop. It was a huge one-story brick building. Hardcore Cycles was brightly lit on a neon sign in white, red, and black colors that hung outside on top of the main entrance doors. Alongside the building was the garage with two bay doors. I walked in through the main entrance to the showroom floor. All different types of motorcycles, from sport bikes, to custom choppers, and older Harleys were parked with sale tags hanging off handlebars.

Skully had told me to look for Torque, the owner and manager. He described him as a big, burly, tattooed biker, and of course, all the men I seemed to be surrounded by fit that description anyway. I heaved a sigh, taking my chances and found one standing behind the service counter, talking to a young teenage girl. He stopped in mid-sentence to look at me, then his mouth dropped open.

"Ah. Are you Torque?" I asked him.

It took him a moment as he blinked. "Yes, darlin', that's me. Are you Skully's girl?"

"I'm not his girl, but I *am* here to see him. Is he here?" I looked around the showroom and figured he was working in the garage.

"Yeah, he's here, he's in the garage, but..."

I gave Torque a smile, took off my shades, and turned toward the front entrance. I figured I'd just go out around the building to find him.

"Wait! Let me go get him for you, okay?" Torque came around the counter, trying to catch up to me.

"That's okay. I'll go out and around." I walked out the front door and headed toward the first garage.

The heavy clouds released their first heavy drops of rain just as I came to the entrance of the first garage. Skully stood next to a bike on the lift, holding a woman in his arms, her back turned to me. He looked up to see me just standing there, frozen. My jaw dropped open as I felt a boulder sink to the bottom of my stomach. I turned away and ran back to my car.

"Tanya! Wait! It's not what you think!" Skully shouted, and he was close behind me. I made it to my car, shut the door, and locked it. He was there, his palms slapped against my window.

The clouds opened up, and rain poured from above, soaking him. "Tanya! Don't go! Let me explain!"

I flipped the bird at him and mouthed the words *fuck you*. I backed my car out, then shifted into drive. My tires spun as I stomped on the gas pedal, peeling out of the Hardcore Cycles parking lot.

I gripped my steering wheel tight with both hands and drove above the speed limit back to my apartment. Tears fell and rolled down my cheeks, ruining my fresh coat of mascara. I made half crescent moon shapes on the inside on my palms. I was so fucking stupid. I wasn't thinking with my head but with my heart and my pussy. I was so pissed! But I was hurt and embarrassed too. He was holding that woman and comforting her. I had barged in feeling like an intruder. *How could Owen explain that away?* Once in my apartment, I poured myself some Moscato. It was pucker sweet going down with my first two sips as I slumped on my couch.

I sat on my couch, balling my eyes out for a half hour when I heard three knocks on my door. "Tanya, it's me, Skully. Will you open the door? I need to talk to you."

After the second glass of wine, I was feeling the effects, and it helped raise my anger up a notch.

I opened my door to see Skully standing there soaking wet, water dripping from his short, messy dark hair.

I waved him and closed the door. "Say what you need to say and make it quick. I don't have time for any bullshit lies either," I snapped.

He stepped inside and spun around to face me, "What you just saw is not what you think it is."

"Then what the fuck is it, Skully? Some chick all up on you like that? And don't say it was your sister—"

"No, it's not my sister. It was Mandi."

"Mandi? She-devil Mandi?"

"Yes. *That* Mandi. She used to be Ratchet's main squeeze, right? She went to Knuck and the Hell Hounds. She's the one who told Sid and Rusty where they could find Sam, at that bookstore she works at. That's how they got to her."

"Why the hell was she there hugging on you?"

He turned away, running a hand through his wet

hair. "She told me she feels bad about it now. She heard that I'm not a Hound anymore. She wants out and to get away from the Hell Hounds too. She seemed sincere and started to cry. I was telling her that it would be okay, and I'd help her figure something out."

I squeezed my eyes shut, and then the images of Matthew came flooding back. Him on his back in our bed ... Fucking Melissa, her huge tits smothering his face.

I hurled my full glass of wine at him. "Get the fuck out."

The glass hit him in the center of his back, crashed to the floor, and shattered into pieces.

He turned back to me and shook his head. "I'm not your ex-douchebag boyfriend. Yeah, I've done some pretty fucked up things, selling drugs, fistfights. But I wouldn't do to you what he did to you. You should come first, remember? And you do come first to me, Tanya. If I walk out, I won't come back. I've been alone all my life. I've been beaten and bullied so many fucking times, I lost count. That's why I joined the Hounds. I was trying to prove something to everyone else. That I had balls. That even though I had a limp, I could pound my fists into any motherfucker who wanted a piece of me. But it made my stomach turn every time I saw how Sid and Rusty abused Sam. The way they treated her—like she was a thing. Not a person. That's what bullies do."

"Why are you telling me this, Skully?"

He moved toward me, grabbing my arms. "Because I don't want to be alone anymore! I've fucked so many women I can't even remember their names or their faces. It was fun, and nothing else. But with you, it's different. It's more than fun. It hurts at first because I'm fucking scared. But when I'm with you, when I'm inside you, I don't hurt anymore. I don't feel alone!"

Too many words were coming out of his mouth. I stood there, frozen, and my eyes welled up with tears again. "Who do you think I am, Owen? Wonder Woman? I'm not even a *whole* woman, for fuck's sake!"

His brows closed in together and I saw the sadness in his dark eyes. He released me, dropping his arms to his sides, and looked down. "You're *my* Wonder Woman." Mumbling, he stepped away and walked out my door.

I cleaned up the shattered wineglass and collapsed back on my couch. I drew my knees up against my chest and broke down. I wasn't angry at Owen, not really; I was mad at myself. He'd shown me again how sweet he can be. How he put me on a pedestal and made me feel like Wonder Woman. That look of need in his eyes when he was inside me. His need for *me*.

As I sobbed, my phone on the coffee table rang. Wez was lit up on the screen. I took a deep breath to compose myself, and then I answered. "Hi, Wez. "

"Hey, Tanya. How's it going, pretty girl?" Wez wore his hair in a mohawk, and his muscled arms were covered in ink, even up along his neck. But his deep, warm voice contradicted his intimidating appearance

"I'm good."

"That's good, baby girl. Is Skully there? He told me he was swinging by your place."

"He just left. How did you know he was coming by?"

"That's why I called. I was riding home on my bike when all hell broke loose. The fuckin' rain nearly drowned me as I was takin' a turn and went down—"

I sat up suddenly from the couch. "Are you okay, Wez?"

"Just a bit of road rash on the elbow. Nothing I can't handle. I was fucked, though. Soaked all the way through to my ass crack, looking like a dumbass trying to pick my bike up. Then a few minutes later, your man, Skully, pulled up on his bike and helped me lift it. I fucked up the brake linkage and scratched up the side of the tank a little. He told me to come by that shop, Hardcore Cycles, and he'd fix it all up for me."

"Oh, thank goodness. I'm glad you're okay, Wez."

"Yeah; me too. Would've sucked balls if I broke some bones. Maybe I'm like a cat with nine lives, huh, pretty girl?" He chuckled.

"Yeah, Wez. You may just be part feline."

"Well, if I am, I'm a fuckin' lion!" More chuckling on his end.

"Skully was here for a few minutes, but he left."

"He's a good dude, Tanya. I know some of my Chaos brothers don't like him much, but he's good with me. Let him know I'll hook him up sometime if he wants some new ink done."

SKULLY

CHAOS KINGS
MOTORCYCLE CLUB

I rode back to my shithole motel in the rain. I wasn't sure how I kept my grip on the handlebars and my throttle open since my whole body was numb. Tanya just got an earful. All of it— my shitty childhood, my shitty life. I felt the familiar painful feeling of being pushed away and not wanted. Alone again. Maybe I was better off being a Hound than being alone.

Tanya hadn't texted or called since I left her apartment. I told Mandi to meet me at the CrowBar two nights later. I got off work and rode to the bar, thanking mother nature for keeping the heavy clouds and rain at bay. Mandi was already there when I kicked my stand down and came in to sit next to her at the bar. The purple bruise under her left eye was a shade lighter than it was when I saw her the other day. She flipped her hair, turning to look at me. She always played that hair-flip routine with other dudes, but it didn't work on me.

"Hi, Skully. How's it hanging? I hope it's heavy..." she purred at me and giggled.

"Cut the crap, Mandi. I'm not here to hook up. I'm here to talk about the reason you came to see me at work the other day."

She turned back to her drink, twirling the little straw in her glass. "Oh, yeah. You're banging Tanya. She looked pissed."

"I'm not here to talk about Tanya either. Don't waste my time. You still want out?" I lit a smoke as a bartender served me a glass of bourbon, neat.

"Yes, I do. The Hounds are hardcore, Skully."

"Yes, they are. But you knew that already. That was your choice. I made that choice to go in too. Patched in. And I made that choice to get out."

Mandi closed her eyes as her mouth turned into a frown and she squealed out a cry. I exhaled a drag of my smoke and reluctantly put my arm around her shoulders. She leaned into me, sobbing. "I did an awful thing, telling Sid so many things about Sam and Ratchet. But I was jealous. I was pissed."

Then it hit me. That's how Rusty got to Tanya that night. I leaned away. "And you told Rusty some things, too, didn't you? Things about Tanya?"

She wiped her runny nose and mascara on her bar napkin. She touched her lips with her fingers, with the look of guilt in her eyes. Guilt only because I figured it all out. I swallowed the last of my bourbon, slamming the glass back on the bar, and turned back to her. "You know what that motherfucker did to her? Fuck, Mandi!" I started to sweat. My muscles tensed up as I clenched my jaw so hard it hurt.

"I'm sorry, Skully. I didn't know what Rusty was going to do."

"From now on, just keep your mouth shut. You've already done enough fucked up damage to the Chaos Kings."

Mandi started up again with the crying, wiping her snotty nose on her wrist. I threw some cash on the bar and was off the stool.

She grabbed my bicep. "But wait, Skully!"

I rolled my eyes and turn back to her. "What? We're done here. Being in that club is different to both of us. I was a club member, and it's not easy to get out of it alive. You're not in it as bad as Sam was. She needed Chaos to get her out. But you, you're better off. Just stay away from the Hounds. Hang with a different crowd."

"You think the Chaos Kings would be good with

me if I made some apologies? Do you think they'd let me come back around?"

"I doubt you'll be welcomed back to Chaos. But an apology is a good start to make it right with them." She let go of my arm, and I walked out of the Crow-Bar, leaving her at the bar to fend for herself.

Another week went by, and I missed Tanya so much it hurt, like a dull physical pain throughout my body. I missed her face, her voice, her soft body. My chest was heavy, and I didn't have much of an appetite. The only thing that kept me in motion was the flow of bikes that needed work during the hot steamy summer month.

Wez pulled in on his custom Harley Softail—a very nice-looking ride, with a flat black tank and fenders. The high ape-hanger bars were black, along with the motor and pipes. It sported a springer front end, with whitewall tires and red wheels. The word HARDCORE was painted in bold white letters on both sides of the tank.

He kicked the stand down, climbed off, and offered me his hand. "Hey, man. That was a better ride than last week, that's for fuckin' sure."

I shook his hand. "Hey, Wez. Yeah, another hot-as-fuck day to ride, though, but better than rain. Are you okay with leaving your bike here for a few days? We can get your tank all spiffed up again and fix that brake linkage for you."

"Yeah. I got a cage I can drive to the tat shop in, so I'm good. I really appreciate this, Skully."

"No problem." I lit a smoke, needing a quick break and to shoot the shit with someone.

"How's it going with you and my pretty girl, Tanya? She is a bossy one, ain't she?" He chuckled, his eyes crinkling at the corners.

"You can say that again. I don't know what's going on anymore. We haven't talked since I stopped by her place that night after I helped you out getting your bike up off the road."

Wez scratched his stubbled jaw. His mohawk was growing out, showing his natural light brown hair color. "Huh. Well. When she wants some more of you, she's got your number."

That's what I was hoping for every minute of the day. I exhaled a drag. "Hey, Wez. Can I ask you something?"

"Yeah, man. What's up?"

"You know I'm out of the club, that I'm not a Hound anymore."

"Yeah. And you made peace with Chaos. But I can't say that all my brothers care too much for you."

"I'm trying to clean up my act. I just landed this legit job here at Hardcore Cycles. But I'm living in a shitty motel in the next county over. I'm trying to rid myself of the bad stain the Hounds left on me. I got some cash saved up. Was wondering if you had any brothers or friends looking for a roommate?"

"Hmm...No." He started rubbing his chin again, staring off.

"Okay. Thanks, Wez. Never hurts to ask, I guess. "

"I tell you what. I'll talk with my brothers. Maybe you could bunk at the clubhouse for a while till you find somewhere to shack up that's better than that motel. You could help out around the place, pay rent to our Treasurer, Shrek."

The weight on my shoulders felt a little bit lighter than it did in the past week. "I owe you, Wez."

"No problem, man. You helped me out the other night. Not many people in this town would stop to help a biker, especially one who looks like a crazy motherfucker who just walked off the set of a Mad Max movie!"

TANYA

CHAOS KINGS
MOTORCYCLE CLUB

Two weeks went by, and no word from Skully. I started a text message several times, but I kept erasing it. I wanted to apologize to him for being such a bitch. And my stomach did flips when my phone buzzed with every incoming text, but they were either from Sam, Honey, or other friends. Sam left me a text that Saturday afternoon a few hours before my shift at the salon was over.

"Hey, sweetie—party tonight at clubhouse—u have 2 be there."

I got home from work, primped, and arrived at the clubhouse for another Saturday night of crazy fun with my tribe. Sam was there, with Ratchet towering over her, his forefinger in the belt loop of her jeans. He was the possessive caveman when it came to his woman. She welcomed me with a warm hug. We squealed and giggled. Her coworker, Kat, was standing next to her. She was all decked out in a long flowy summer dress with flowers and flip flops. She wore black-rimmed glasses; her hair dyed a bold purple. She was as cute as a button, just like Sam.

I pulled her into a warm embrace, squeezing her. "Is this your first time at a Chaos party, Kat?"

"Yes, my first time." She blushed, but her eyes were focused on something behind me. I turned to see Magnet over at the pool tables, playing cutthroat with two hot blondes, of course.

"Magnet has that effect on women. But not me. I grew up with that boy. It's best you just admire him from a distance, Kat. He's a player."

She tore her eyes away from Magnet and back at me, with her jaw open, and her eyes as big as saucers. "What's his name?"

"Noah. But we all call him Magnet. Like chick magnet?"

"That name suits him well," she replied with a slight blush to her cheeks.

I cracked up. I should have known Magnet would have that effect on her too. When I turned back to look at him, I caught sight of Skully as he stood next to Wez, smoking a cigarette and drinking a beer. Then his eyes met mine, and he nodded as his mouth lifted in a smile. His eyes went back to Wez as he conversed with him.

"Who invited Skully?" I hoped someone would answer quickly.

"He's shacking up here for a while. Chaos had a meet with him a week ago. The Prez and VP are good with it. He's helping out here like Sam did once. And he's paying rent to Shrek," Ratchet informed me.

I walked behind the bar and grabbed myself a beer from the stocked fridge. I twisted off the cap, and the first swallow was nice and cold. My stomach did one of those same flips every time I caught sight of Skully, but I didn't know whether to approach him first or wait for him to come to me. I shook my head and drank another mouthful, feeling the refreshment of the cold brew going down and goading me on.

You can do this, Tanya. I thought to myself. *You want to apologize to him for being shitty, then go over there and do it...Here goes.*

So, I did just that, and Skully watched me as I approached. Wez's back was facing me, and he turned to see what Skully was smiling at.

Then Wez reached out and wrapped his big burly arms around me. He kissed my cheek. "How's my pretty girl today?"

I wrapped my arms around his waist. "I'm good, Wez. I need a drink, and I need some fun tonight. It's so good to be here with my tribe. Hi, Skully. Good to see you too." I smiled at him as Wez embraced me.

He smiled, tipping his bottle at me. "Good to see you too, Tanya. Pretty in pink. As always."

Wez coughed, clearing his throat. "I'm empty and need to drain the dragon." He walked away, leaving us alone, surrounded by the sound of pool balls whacking into each other and loud music blaring from the jukebox.

I swallowed the lump in my throat before I could speak again. "I want to apologize for last week, Owen. I was a total shit. Will you forgive me?"

He stepped toward me. "No apology is needed. I want to thank you for listening. It was too much, and I didn't mean to dump all of that on you. And I'm sorry if I pissed you off about Mandi."

"No need. That was just my own insecurity rearing its ugly head. I need to reel that in. My breakup with Matthew did a killing to my self-esteem, which makes me have trust issues when it comes to men."

Skully dropped his smoke, crushed it with his boot, and slid his hand into his jeans pocket. "That douchebag should be the one with self-esteem and trust issues. Not you. You're a wonder of a woman, Tanya. His loss. And hopefully, my gain..."

My throat hurt as I choked back tears. "Do you want to start over again with us? Because I do."

He leaned in and kissed me gently. "Yes, Tanya. I do want to start over again. With you."

Butterflies fluttered their little wings in my stomach when he spoke those words.

We enjoyed the rest of the night together at the clubhouse. We slammed down a few Fireball shots with Ratchet and Sam, and Wez played cut-throat pool with Skully and me. When it was my turn at the pool table, I'd leaned down and took my aim behind the cue ball. Then I arched my back just a bit and wiggled my ass. Wez and Skully both focused on it as I took my shot. Both of them winced as the number three ball dropped into the corner pocket, making me the winner of the game.

The Fireball shots and several beers began to bring out the brave and slutty Tanya. I grabbed the front of Skully's T-shirt, pulling him to me and shoved my tongue into his mouth before he could blink twice.

"Gotta go drain the dragon ... Again." I barely heard what Wez said behind me because I was still latched onto Skully. He wrapped his arms around my waist and pressed himself against me. He was rock hard. He wanted me.

He leaned away, breaking our kiss. "I *need* you, Tanya." His deep voice was sending tingles straight to my clit.

"Then let's ride back to my apartment. I'll give you what you need, Skully."

Skully road us on his bike at full throttle back to my apartment. Once inside, I held his hand, leading him to my couch before pushing him down into it. I lowered myself onto my knees and began to undo his jeans. His brows shot up, and the pace of his breathing sped up.

"Just relax. I'll make the hurt go away." I yanked his jeans down a bit, pulling him down toward me so that he slouched even further. His hard cock sprang free.

I wrapped my hand around him and flicked my tongue several times over the thick, juicy head. He gasped then groaned. "Fuck, Tanya!"

"Yeah, that's what you're going to do to me, all right." I wrapped my lips around his thick length, and my head bobbed as I sucked and drooled all over him.

I tormented, teased, and tasted his hardness, getting it slippery wet with my tongue. I released him and stood up, kicking off my wedge heels and shimmied out of my tight jeans and panties. I climbed on him, lowering myself until I was impaled to the hilt with his smooth thickness. I cried out as he gripped my hips, bucking and grinding to match my rhythm. He bit his lower lip, as he looked up and our eyes met; his were glossed over and filled with a hungry yearning. He touched me in just the right spot against my clit, and the orgasm rose and washed over me.

"Yes, Tanya. God, you're so fucking beautiful!" He let out a primal growl as he came with me. He exploded as my walls contracted, squeezing him as he pulsated deep inside me.

SKULLY

CHAOS KINGS
MOTORCYCLE CLUB

My Wonder Woman collapsed on me, panting and sweating. I was breathing hard and fast, along with her. I wrapped my arms around her. We didn't move, basking in our intense release.

"I got pregnant with Matthew. But I miscarried." It was just a whisper, her breath on my chest, but I heard it.

I squeezed her tighter. "I'm sorry, Tanya."

"But that's only half of it. And I guess I deserved it—finding him fucking Melissa in our bed. Then moving out and leaving me afterward."

"No, you didn't deserve any of that. That douche wasn't man enough for you."

She rose to look into my eyes, her brows drawn together. "I had an abortion when I was seventeen,

Owen. The only one who knows about it is Magnet. And now you. So, yeah, I did deserve it."

I sat up, keeping my arms wrapped around her. "No, you didn't! Is that what you think? I'm sorry you had to go through something like that when you were so young. I'm glad you had Magnet to be there for you, to help you get through it. You're not a bad person if that's what you're thinking. You are a brave, sassy, beautiful woman. You had to make a grown-up decision at such a young age. And your miscarriage? I don't know much about those kinds of things. But who knows, maybe it was just not meant to be. I was an orphan. My parents gave me up when I was just starting to walk. I don't even remember them. They didn't want me. But maybe that was meant to be too. Maybe I was better off living in foster homes and having a guardian of the state. Maybe things like this just happen. Think about it. I would never have met you that night if I didn't help Sam. I made that choice too. And I'm happy I did."

She tilted her head, and I cupped her wet cheek in the palm of my hand. "Maybe you're right, Owen. The world can be so fucked up and chaotic sometimes. But we make our own choices."

"And I'm here for you. I'm at your beck and call. Anytime. Anywhere. Besides, your Chaos brother,

Wez, gave me some good advice when it comes to you too."

"And what advice was that?"

"That you're a bit bossy. That I should do whatever it is you want."

She leaned her head back and began to laugh. "Yeah. I admit it. I *am* the bossy type. You think you can handle it, Skully?"

"I know I can. I need to be told what to do anyway. To keep me steering in the right direction."

Make-up sex with Tanya for the past few weeks just blew me away. We wore each other out! She drained me to the point that it made my limp more noticeable to everyone. The guys at the bike shop gave me a tough time, too, telling me I had my hands full. I agreed with them, but I didn't let them know it.

I kept up the Chaos clubhouse when I got off work, even helping the girls out behind the bar to keep the club members happy with beer and shots. The room I chose to bunk in was way better than the shithole motel room I'd stayed in.

The boss man, Torque, was cool enough to let me work out my schedule to match Tanya's. I'd pick her up on my bike and take her for a ride on our days off together. The summer season was still hot, but the sticky air pushing against us as we rode felt so good. She would lean back on the sissy bar, wearing her white-rimmed shades, and I'd admire her from the side mirror.

One morning, I rode her to a different coffee shop. And this time, we finished off our coffee and talked. We'd ride on backroads, the shade from the trees covered us from the hot sun. We'd either stop in at the clubhouse or end up back at her apartment. Sometimes, after some hardcore sex, she'd let me sleep in her bed overnight. I would lie awake until she'd fall asleep, listening to her soft little snores. It was fucking adorable.

I called up Wez and made an appointment to get some ink done to cover up a particular tat—the Hell Hounds MC. That old saying sometimes seems true, you'll regret getting this tat, or that tat someday. Well, I regretted the Hounds tat that stared up at me every day. Wez and his partners named the shop Mad Ink. I walked into the intoxicating scent of ink and the buzzing sound of the tattoo guns wafting through the air. Flash art covered every wall in the place, from old school to basic skulls, pirates, animals, butterflies, and flowers. Wez'spartner was bent over a woman as she lay across a bench, working a design with his ink gun on her upper thigh.

Wez sat at his station, preparing his ink gun, noticing my limp as I came to sit next to him. He chuckled. "Damn, Skully. Does pretty girl ever let you up for air? Or does she just keep you chained to her bed?"

I shoved my hands into my pockets, feeling a little embarrassed. I knew Wez would pick up on my limp, despite my always trying to keep it as unnoticed as possible. "Yeah. Sometimes she does." That got another chuckle out of him.

I decided on a dragon with just black ink for the shading and Wez got to work on covering the Hell Hound tat. The buzzing sound of the ink gun pulled me into a trance, even though it hurt like a son of a bitch. The pain released endorphins throughout my body, drowning out everything around me.

I kept still, solid as a rock as Wez's gun tore through my skin. "So, how's your ride? Did I fix it up okay with the new linkage?"

He was steady with the gun, concentrating on my forearm. "Yeah, man. She rides and purrs really good for me. I really appreciate it. Are ya likin' the clubhouse better than the shithole motel?"

"Yeah. I like it. I can't thank you enough. Can

you put a good word in for me to Chaos about my mechanic skills with bikes? Your Chaos brothers can bring them by Hardcore Cycles. I'll make sure they get great service."

Wez stopped his torture on my flesh, turning to dip the gun back into the black ink. "Ever thought of prospecting for Chaos?"

Prospecting? The last time I prospected was with the Hounds. It wasn't a pleasant experience, but it's what you had to do before becoming a patched in member for a diamond club. "I'd need a sponsor. But what about your brothers? Don't think they'd want an ex-member of the Hell Hounds in their club."

"I know Magnet's not too fond of you, but that's only because Tanya is like a sister to him. None of the other brothers have any beef with you, though. You pretty much saved Ratchet's ol' lady from being sold off to a bunch of Russian mob pukes. You helped me out and got my bike purring like a fine-tuned machine. You could be a good addition to Chaos. And the bonus is pretty girl, Tanya. She never lets you see daylight anyway, at least when you're alone with her. I'll be your sponsor."

Two days later, I made sure the clubhouse bar was well stocked, and I knew what the club members' favorite drink of choice were, whether beer or liquor or weed. Wez pulled in on his Softail before the others rolled in that night. I handed him a nice cold beer as he admired the new dragon tat that covered all remnants of the Hell Hounds. Rocky walked in with his VP, Spider, first, then Ratchet, Gunner and Magnet. The rest rolled in, parking their bikes side by side a few minutes later.

"So, you wanna prospect for Chaos." Rocky's arms were folded, his stance wide, brooding at me.

I swallowed the lump in my throat. "Yes, I do, Prez."

"Prospecting for Chaos is a whole different ball game. It's not the same as prospecting for a diamond club. You pay your dues, pay attention, and do as you're told. The tasks you perform for any patched in member, you give it a hundred percent. You're only a prospect and will be addressed that way. You're expected to learn all club members' names, what they do for a living, what they like, what they hate. Your main focus will be security detail. You're expected to be there for all rides. Getting there early will earn you brownie points. You'll also be expected to watch over club members' bikes. And the most important task of all—escorting ol' ladies and the women in the coven. They are to be treated with respect – at all times. A club member won't tell you to perform a task that they wouldn't do themselves. Remember that. Wez is your sponsor. Learn from him. And don't disappoint. Got it?"

"Yes, Prez. I'm ready to do this."

TANYA

CHAOS KINGS
MOTORCYCLE CLUB

I heard Skully's pipes before he pulled into my apartment parking lot. I was giddy as I looked out my window. I smiled, remembering the last time we were together. Holding on to him while he rode me on the bike. He came over, and we sat on the couch together watching *Mad Max: Fury Road*. I popped some popcorn in the microwave but got distracted and put the movie on pause, as we both started shedding our clothes right there in my kitchen. He fucked me as I bent over the kitchen counter. He thrust himself inside me, filling me up. He gripped my hips, breathing heavily against my ear, telling me how wet and soft I felt. He grabbed hold of my hair, and I cried out, my back arched. I instantly reached the brink of an exhilarating orgasm. He then rode a wave of pleasure as his hot cum squirted deep inside me. The plastic bowl of warm popcorn was knocked off the edge of the counter, crashing on the floor and scattering its contents everywhere.

We worked long hours the whole week, so we were only able to talk on the phone and text when we could catch a break. The texting would turn into sexting, starting with how my pink panties were soaked through thinking of him all day. And how it wasn't easy for him to recalibrate a bike when his dick was rock hard for me.

It wasn't until he kicked his stand down in the parking lot and climbed off the bike that I noticed his new black leather vest. He was grinning from ear to ear when I opened my door. "I'm prospecting for Chaos, sweet cheeks." He snatched me up in his arms, lifting me off my feet, and planted a warm kiss on my lips.

"Put me down, I wanna see! Turn around." There it was. The Prospect patch was sewn in along the bottom of his vest.

He turned back around, still grinning. "Wez is my sponsor. I'm doing this, Tanya, becoming Chaos —someday. Hopefully soon."

My heart skipped a beat as my nipples hardened with excitement. I leaped back into his arms, wrapping mine over his solid shoulders, and crushed my mouth against his. I felt weightless as he held me and his tongue devoured me. He leaned away. "I'll make you proud, Tanya."

"I'm already proud of you, Owen. You'll become part of my tribe. "

SKULLY

CHAOS KINGS
MOTORCYCLE CLUB

"**Y**ou'll be on your own tonight, so show Chaos what you got, Skully." Wez's big hand was planted on my shoulder, his look intense.

That night was my first legit prospecting job for the Chaos Kings. Tanya got promoted as co-manager for her boss, Honey, at the hair salon. I was so proud of her, along with everyone else. And the President's ol' lady, Madge, wanted to celebrate her birthday. The Chaos Coven were all going out to celebrate, and I was the prospect who would be on escort duty all night.

Some of the Chaos brothers hung around the clubhouse, as they waited on the women to show up. I was given rules to follow and was told what was expected of me that night. Ratchet was in a very dark mood, and I couldn't blame him. Sam was invited, and I could sense that he was struggling with himself over his own possessiveness of her.

He took a shot of whiskey at the bar and jabbed a finger into my chest. "Don't let Sam or any of the coven out of your sight. Watch over them every fuckin' second. If something happens to any of them, you'll have to answer to all my brothers and me. Got that, Prospect?"

With his finger jabbing into the center of my chest, I had to concentrate on my stance, hoping I wouldn't be thrown off balance. I sure as hell didn't want to piss any of them off, especially Ratchet. He was a big motherfucker, and I didn't want to experience that forearm of his against my throat ever again. "Understood, Ratchet. I intend to."

Headlights from a black stretch limo beamed through the bay door. The limo driver was ten minutes early. Kat pulled in with Sam, and Tanya had Honey and Madge riding with her. I got a semi hard-on just watching Tanya walk toward me. She had a fresh coat of pink lip gloss on those luscious lips, reminding me again how her mouth did crazy things to my dick. Her black bra showed through her hot pint sheer tank top and did wonders to her cleavage. Her stone washed jeans were tight as fuck and her wedge sandals emphasized the sway of her hips.

"I like that effect I have on you, Skully." Her voice was husky as she wrapped her arms around my neck, giving me a sweet lip-smacking kiss.

I grabbed hold her hips, pulling her to me. I captured her mouth, driving my tongue between her lips. Her little moan suddenly got my dick standing to attention. "Yes, you do affect me, Sweet Cheeks." My growl was low, meant only for her.

She kept her soft, warm body pressed to mine. Both arms were now wrapped around my shoulders. But her smile faded. "Are you okay with doing this tonight by yourself?"

I smirked, and my body relaxed, now that she was there with me. "Yes, babe. I can do this. I already got an earful from Ratchet, Wez, and the other brothers. For the first time, I feel good about doing something legit. To watch over you and the coven. Yeah, I *want* to do this."

The women climbed into the black limo, and I followed on my bike to an outdoor tiki bar along the Potomac River. Tiki torches were lit outside in warm, humid air. I followed close behind the women as they made their way to the horseshoe bar. The beat of club music pounded through speakers. The place was packed, and the night was still early.

Madge bought the first round of fruity shooters for the coven, and Tanya handed me a shot glass full of whiskey. "I want you to do a shot with us to get this night started!" I didn't argue with her, and I downed it as they downed their girly red shooters and hooted and hollered.

I placed my hand on Tanya's lower back and leaned down to whisper in her ear. "Now it's time for me to do my job. Have fun tonight, Sweet Cheeks. I'll be right here."

They huddled close together, next to the bar, giggling and doing another round of shooters. I stood only a few yards away and kept watch. The bartenders kept the flow of drinks coming. Tanya and Madge started to dance with each other, catching the attention of male onlookers. Sam was a bit more subdued, and I guessed it was because this kind of fun was new to her. She was a brave one. Her friend Kat seemed new to this too. But the more they drank, the more they loosened up and laughed along with Tanya and Madge.

Watching Tanya's sexy little body move and the sound of her giggles was a nice distraction. But I had to focus on watching over out for all of them. I stood near them, folding my arms across my chest and zoned in on any man or woman who got too close to them. I couldn't help but crack a smile a few times, overhearing Madge tell some filthy sex jokes, bringing on squeals and giggles from the coven.

Two hours later, I paid their tab and followed the limo to another bar a few miles away. This one was indoors, dimly lit with colorful strobe lights swimming over the dance floor and the sweaty dancing bodies. The place was packed with more people than the tiki bar we just left. I followed close behind them as Madge led the way. We weaved through the packed crowd of sweaty bodies to the bar. Madge got a bartender's attention, yelling her order of drinks over the loud music. I took another whiskey shot with them again as Sam and Kat giggled, their alcohol consumption helping to make them feel more comfortable.

Kat cupped her hand close to Sam's ear, saying something that made her laugh. And that's when it happened. The act was quick that no one noticed, but to me, it was in slow motion. A man's hand grabbed a handful of Sam's ass. That fucking hand was attached to a young white-collar type, douchebag, his sleeves rolled up to his elbows.

Three steps, and within seconds, I moved to

stand behind him. Sam whipped around to see who the idiot was that just touched her. My hand shot out, grabbing an earlobe and twisted. Hard. He let out a high-pitched cry, and his knees buckled.

"Apologize to the lady! Now, motherfucker!" I growled into his other ear. His buddy stood to the other side of him and turned to look my way. I glared right at him. "Don't."

He didn't.

"I'm sorry!" White-collar boy squealed out to Sam, her eyes glaring up into his.

I twisted the earlobe again just a notch, and he squealed again. "Now I just saved your life, dumbass. Her ol' man is a Chaos King. If he found out what you just did, he'd cut you up into little pieces and keep a few of your body parts as trophies. Now, get the fuck out of my sight!"

Douchebag squealer was gone, as his buddy followed close behind, maneuvering through the crowd. I turned back to Sam.

She was smiling at me. "Thanks, Skully. You're not going to tell Ratchet, are you?"

"Hell, no! It'll be much worse for me than what *that* motherfucker just got. It's my job to keep all of you safe tonight. So, no, it can stay between us. Is that okay with you?"

"Yes. And you *are* keeping us safe tonight. I wouldn't be able to have any fun if we didn't have Chaos watching over us."

"I'm not a Chaos King. I'm just a prospect."

"But you *will* be a Chaos King someday, Skully. I know you will."

Tanya placed her hand on my shoulder. "What happened?"

"Some asshole just did a stupid thing and touched Sam. But after tonight, his earlobe is going to need some fuckin' stitches."

"Oh, my god, Sam. Are you okay?"

"Yeah. I'm okay, Tanya. Skully took care of him," Sam replied, beaming a pretty smile.

TANYA

CHAOS KINGS
MOTORCYCLE CLUB

Even after what just happened, Sam didn't want to leave the bar just yet. So, we stayed, and Skully kept his watch over us as we finished off a few more drinks and danced. My feet hurt like a son of a bitch from the standing and dancing all night long. It was midnight by the time Skully paid our tab, and we all climbed back into the limo and to the clubhouse. Despite the incident with Sam, the coven had a fun time. We giggled, with Madge telling us dick jokes on the way back to the clubhouse. I kicked off my sandals and switched on the tiny lights that ran alongside the interior of the limo.

I was horny as hell all night long for Skully, just knowing I was safe and the coven was protected. He was always nearby, with his arms crossed over his hard chest, wearing his prospect patch. Often, our eyes met, and the side his mouth lifted in a smirk, as we both had dirty thoughts running through our minds, knowing just how good we made each other feel. I would picture him wearing the full Chaos Kings MC patch, and my panties were soaked.

The limo driver took us back to the clubhouse and gave both Madge and Honey a ride home. I wanted to stay the night with Skully at the clubhouse, and I was in no shape to drive.

We were alone in the room he slept in, and I stripped off my clothes as fast as I could. I fell back onto the bed, my arms above my head. I was totally naked. I arched my back and purred, "Can you leave your cut on while you fuck me, Owen?"

His eyes roamed over my body, and he had begun to take off his cut, but stopped and shrugged it back on. "Sure, baby. I'll keep the cut on as I pound my hard dick deep into that sweet pussy of yours."

He undid his jeans and shoved them down to reveal that sexy V-shape of his hips. His cock sprung free, and he covered my body with his. I inhaled his male scent as his lips latched onto my neck. His wet tongue darted out to taste my skin. His lips nipped and sucked, bringing goose bumps to rise along my entire body. I gasped as his teeth clamped down and bit me right at the juncture of my neck and shoulder.

"My dick has been hard all night for you." He groaned against my neck, making my nipples so hard, they ached.

"Well, what are you waiting for? Give it to me."

He gripped his thick rod and sank it inside me as I cried out. He fed me what I was hungry for all night long. He raised himself above me and pinned my wrists down to the bed. His hips began to grind, his cock stretching me, filling me. "Here you go, baby. Take all of me."

My hips bucked and writhed in rhythm with his as he pounded into me. His mouth covered mine, muffling my cries and moans. His hips ground and rubbed against my swollen nub.

"Yeah, baby. Come on my cock!" his deep, warm voice commanded, and my climax was so intense, I screamed. We looked into each other's eyes as my orgasm pulsated around him. He groaned, his voice low and thick with emotion. He spasmed inside me as he climaxed, before he collapsed on top of me, releasing my wrists. I wrapped my arms around him, trying to steady my breathing.

"I want to fall asleep just like this," I whispered

breathlessly. Then his breathing grew even and steady, matching mine.

"That's what happens to girls like you."

Another sharp painful cramp rocked me to my core. It's dark. I was freezing. I wrapped myself in my arms as I buckled and leaned over with the onslaught of more pain.

Wetness. I raised my hands. Wet, dark blood covered them.

"Tanya, baby. Wake up." Owen's husky voice penetrated through my sleepy dream. My eyes flew open. He was perched on his elbow, looking down at me, his brows drawn together.

Another painful cramp. I shut my eyes tight, but the tears came. I sat up suddenly and ripped the blanket that covered us. Dried blood caked my inner thighs to match the dark stain underneath me. Owen saw it too. His hand reached up to cup my cheek. "It's okay, baby. Let me get something for you." He climbed out of bed and went down the hall to the bathrooms. He returned and lay back in the bed next to me with a warm, wet washcloth. He began to wipe the dried blood from my thighs.

My hand shot out to stop him. "Don't."

"It's okay. I know some guys freak out about women's periods. Not me, though. It's one of those magical things about women. It's nature. Just relax."

I let go of his hand, and he continued to rub the warm cloth on my thighs. It was comforting and brought me back from the bad dream. I wiped tears away with the palms of my hands. "Sometimes, when I get the awful cramps, they haunt me in my dreams. A reminder of the pain. The abortion. The miscarriage."

He leaned in and pecked my temple with soft kisses. It soothed me.

Then I remembered I had a morning shift to work at the salon. "Shit! I'm going to be late. And I just got this promotion!"

"You're going to call in sick today, and I'll drive you back to your place. I don't want you on your feet all day, dealing with those cramps." I didn't argue with him. I really wanted to be in my bed, and I wanted him in it with me.

I called Honey and told her I was having one of those days. She was a bit hungover from the night before too, but she said that she'd work the salon for the day with the other stylists. I gave Owen my car keys, and he drove me back to my apartment. He said he'd take care of the sheets and would also take the day off to spend it with me.

SKULLY

CHAOS KINGS
MOTORCYCLE CLUB

Two months had passed, and I was proving myself to the Chaos Kings as a prospect. I showed up for rides with the club at least thirty minutes early. Club members came to me when they needed help with their bikes. Sam and I kept it on the DL over what happened at the bar that night, and she even put a good word in for me to Ratchet.

I was on time with my clubhouse dues and rent to the treasurer, Shrek. He was a big hulk of a man, as big as Ratchet, except he was more laid back and easy-going, and he didn't wear a brooding scowl on his face. He liked to joke around, but when things got serious, he did too.

It was another Friday night, and I was stocking the beer fridge and the liquor shelves. I knew what each member liked to drink and made sure the clubhouse was fully stocked. The sun was lowering behind the trees in the parking lot as a few of the Chaos brothers started pulling in and parking their bikes.

Shrek had been there for a while as he stood at the jukebox, pushing buttons on the screen with his thick fingers, scrolling through the alphabetized song list. His mouth was clamped down on half a cigar, and he looked irritated. "What the fuck, prospect? What happened to my song "Say Fuck It" by Buckcherry?"

I wiped down the bar with a wet rag, emptying out ashtrays. "I don't know, Shrek. The jukebox dude was here last week. I guess he changes up the song lists on that thing."

Shrek turned to face me. "Goddammit, prospect! Call that motherfucker and tell him to put it back on here!" Something was wrong. I'd never seen him get so wound up over something as trivial as a song on the jukebox. "Fuck it," he said, pushing a button for a different song. He headed over to the bar, grabbed a stool, and sat in front of me.

"I'll call him today to get that song back on there for you."

"Pour me some tequila, prospect," he grumbled. I turned to grab a bottle of his favorite and heard the thunder of more bikes pulling into the lot. Some were noisier than usual, revving their throttles, as they parked alongside each other. The Chaos Kings were ready to throw down a few that night.

I came from around the bar as they marched in together, Rocky in the lead. They all glared right at me with pissed-off expressions on their faces. *What were they pissed at—me?* I didn't know, but it sure as hell felt like it.

Wez reached me first, socking me in the shoulder. "Just keep your mouth shut, prospect."

"You fucked up, prospect!" Rocky barked, moving past Wez to stand an inch away from my nose. He didn't blink, just glared into my eyes.

I wasn't sure how I fucked up, but I didn't want to piss the Prez off more than he already was. So, I did as Wez told me—I kept my mouth shut. But my jaw clenched. Rocky just stood there for only a few seconds, but it felt like a whole fucking hour. Then he blinked and the sides of his eyes crinkled as he chuckled. "Just bustin' your balls, prospect. You looked like you were gonna shit your pants!" His head flew back, chuckling even louder.

I exhaled loudly, not realizing I was holding my breath. "Could have, I guess."

"Did you have a hearty nutritional breakfast, lunch, and dinner today?"

Rocky and everyone else was acting so fucking strange. Then he grabbed me by the shoulders with his beefy hands. "Cause as of this very moment, you're not a prospect anymore, Skully. You're now a fully patched-in member of the Chaos Kings. You're our brother now."

Wez held out the two patches that made up the Chaos Kings Motorcycle Club patch; the top with Chaos Kings and the center with a grinning skull wearing a Viking helmet, set above two crossed battle axes.

Wez had a shit-eating grin on his face as I took the patches from him. My throat felt dry, and I swallowed, hoping I wouldn't lose it in front of them. I was a club member now. A brother. A Chaos King.

"It's good you ate something today because tonight is your patch-in party, brother. Don't disappoint." *Wez called me brother.*

I knew it was going to be a long night celebrating. Shots were passed around at the clubhouse, then we rose to the Cheetah Club where I received several lap dances, thanks to my Chaos brothers. And I knew it would somehow get back to Tanya, but I hoped that she would be okay with it.

TANYA

CHAOS KINGS
MOTORCYCLE CLUB

S am had texted me early in the day that Ratchet told her to get the word out to the coven that we all were going to celebrate Skully becoming a Chaos King. I was handling a customer at the register and squealed when I read her text. I hurried back to my apartment after work, took a quick shower, primped and got dressed to get to the clubhouse by eleven o'clock.

Skully had been the poster boy of what a good prospect was supposed to be. He put the Chaos brothers before himself every day. He put me on that pedestal too. He even helped out as a road captain on some of the rides; I was so proud to sit on the back of his bike. Sometimes, he would look at me like I was the center of his world—his eyes all fiery and gleaming, making me feel like the most beautiful woman in the world. When I was with Matthew, he'd made me feel like I was biker trash. Skully made me feel like I was a hot-as-fuck biker babe.

I picked up Sam on the way to the clubhouse. She had never been to a patch in party, and she was just as excited as I was. I'd been to a few and knew Skully would have to pull through his first night partying hard as a Chaos King. I knew his brothers would take him to one of the local strip clubs, and yes, I knew he would get plenty of lap dances. I felt just a little sting of jealousy, picturing beautiful naked women rubbing all over him. But I also knew it was only part of the celebration. Owen was Chaos now. And I had a permanent smile on my face driving to the clubhouse.

The coven arrived first, along with Magnet's two blonde friends with benefits, Brandy and Becky. They stood together at the jukebox picking out songs. They were both pretty with curvy figures; BFFs who clung to Magnet on the weekends. I'd only spoken to them a few times, and they seemed okay and just kept to themselves except for being touchy-feely with Magnet. Sam and I went behind the bar, handing out beers and filling up shot glasses for the coven. Then we heard the loud roar of pipes as the Chaos Kings pulled in a few minutes later.

I took a shot of Patrón as Skully walked in. His

limp was a bit more noticeable, only because he was already pretty shit-faced. The red lipstick on his cheek was the next thing I noticed as he stood in front of me with a wide grin on his face.

"You're going to have to rub that lipstick off your cheek before I congratulate you, Skully," I said.

He raked both his hands through his short messy dark hair, looking down at his boots. "Ah...Yeah... Sorry about that, Sweet Cheeks..."

I couldn't keep a straight face anymore and snorted out a giggle. "It's okay. I know what happens at these patch-in parties." I grabbed fistfuls of his T-shirt and pulled him to me, claiming his mouth. "Congratulations, Skully. You're a Chaos King now."

He wrapped his arms around me and staggered a little bit too. "Thanks, Tanya. I belong here with Chaos. I belong here with you." And at that moment, I realized that it was true. He did belong with me.

I leaned away. "I wanna go mess with Magnet and Wez." I grabbed his hand, leading him over to the pool tables where Wez and Gunner were setting up a game.

"Hey, my pretty girl." Wez pulled me into his hard chest, giving me a warm bear hug.

"Did you all have fun tonight getting your new brother all shit-faced? And how many tits were smashed into his face tonight at the Cheetah Club?" I sounded as serious as I could, but my eyes couldn't hide my smile.

"*Plenty* of tits! Tits galore!" Wez chuckled.

I looked over at Gunner as he stood chalking his cue stick, seeming deep in his own world. Wez reached over and sucker-punched him in the shoulder.

He stumbled back. "What the fuck man?"

Wez pointed two fingers at Gunner's eyes, then back to his own. "Where the fuck you at, man? Still thinking about that delicious red-haired siren at the Cheetah?"

Gunner raked a hand through his dark hair. "Yeah, yeah, yeah. Are we playing a game of serious money betting pool here, asshole, or are you just gonna play with your own dick?"

Wez's head fell back, and he let out a loud booming laugh, then leaned down to mumble in my ear. "Gunner was mesmerized by a red-haired beauty dancing at the Cheetah Club tonight. He's probably still sportin' a chubby." He planted a sloppy kiss on my forehead, grabbed his pool stick, and broke the first game of pool. I watched as the cue ball smacked into the triangular set of colored balls, scattering them all over the table. Gunner did seem a little distracted. We all knew he loved looking at beautiful women, but he just admired them from a distance. And he did like the color red. His Road King was cherry red. *Maybe the red-haired exotic dancer captured his attention.*

I left Gunner and Wez to their game and walked with Skully back to the bar. The coven circled him, and we all shared a shot of tequila to celebrate. Then we passed him around the giggling circle, planting heavy caked-on red lipstick kisses on his face. By the time he staggered back to me, he was grinning from ear to ear, lipstick stains covering both cheeks, chin, and even a few on his forehead.

Long after midnight, Skully couldn't walk straight and was stumbling everywhere, looking like a toddler learning to take his first steps. I led him into his room, and he crash-landed on his bed and was out cold the moment his head hit the pillow. I took off his books and lifted his legs onto the bed. I stripped off all my clothes, pulled on one of his T-shirts and climbed into bed next to him.

TANYA

CHAOS KINGS
MOTORCYCLE CLUB

I walked on clouds the next few weeks after Skully's patch-in party. I was so proud of him. He was loyal to the Chaos Kings and faithful to me. Even Magnet warmed up to him a little more, to the point they tinkered with Magnet's bike together at the clubhouse one day, talking motorcycles like most bikers do. Skully stayed the night at my apartment more often too. We took lunch breaks together; sometimes he'd pick me up at the salon on his bike and we'd ride somewhere for a bite to eat, or I would drive over to the bike shop and bring lunch to him.

It was early afternoon when I parked at the shop, bringing Italian subs to share with him. Torque was behind the sales counter talking to someone I couldn't see, and I thought he was just mumbling to himself. I reached the counter and placed the bag of subs on it. "Hey, Torque. I brought lunch for Skully. Is he in the garage?" I tiptoed and leaned over the counter to see who he was talking to.

It was a little boy. He was talking to Torque but stopped and looked at me. His dark hair looked like it was just freshly combed. He wore a black T-shirt with a little skull on it, blue jeans and black chucks. He held two toy motorcycles, a green one, and a red one in his chubby little hands. He smiled, and I smiled back, tilting my head. It was something about his eyes that looked familiar.

"Hey, buddy! How are you? You like motorcycles?" He nodded, still smiling. "Well, you came to the right place!" I kept my smile but turned to look at Torque. "Who's your little friend, Torque?"

Torque tore his eyes away from the boy and looked at me, looking like a deer caught in headlights. At least he was smiling too, though. "Hi, Tanya. This is Jacob—"

"I like to be called Jake," the boy interrupted.

"Well, my name is Tanya. Pleased to meet you, Jake." I leaned over the counter and reached out to shake his little hand. He shook mine, pumping his hand up and down a few times.

I released Jake's hand and stood back up and looked at Torque "Where're his parents?"

He shrugged his shoulders, nodding to someone behind me. "I guess that's his mother. She asked for Skully."

Just then, a woman pushed open the door that leads to the garage. She was slim and tall with blonde hair, wearing tight jeans, and sporting a lot of cleavage from a tank top that fit her a little too tight. Her brows were knitted together, and she looked angry. Then her eyes met mine for a brief second.

Skully came through the same door, right behind her. "Wait, Brittany!" She spun around to look at him. "At least give me some goddamn info! Phone numbers, address? Things like that?"

Brittany grabbed the notepad and pen he was holding and began to scribble something.

She pressed the pen and pad on his chest. "Info's all there. It's your turn, Owen. I need a fuckin' break. Good luck." Brittany stormed toward the front door with a brisk walk.

"Mom?" Jake came from around the counter, running to catch up to her. She turned around and kneeled down to look directly at him. "Stay with Skully today, sweetie. He'll take you over to Grandma's later, okay?"

"Where are you going, Mom? I don't know him

or them either." He turned his head to look at the three of us.

"He's one of the good guys, Jake. You're safe with him. Stay with him and don't go anywhere with other grown-ups, okay?"

"Okay, Mom." Jake's shoulders slumped a bit. He wrapped his little arms around Brittany's neck, and she squeezed him back. Then she walked out the front door and was gone. He turned around slowly, still holding the little motorcycles in his hands. His head titled and he looked sad and confused.

Skully took a step and smiled. "Hey, Jake, you wanna come and check out the garage with Tanya and me? There's a bike in there that I'm working on."

Jake's eyes lit up, and he walked toward us. "Okay! That would be really coo-wall!" and reached up to take Skully's hand.

Skully took Jake's little hand in his and turned to me. "Coming with us, Tanya?"

"Sure." I kept a smile on my face even though a rock felt like it sunk down to the pit of my stomach. I followed them through the door to the garage to see a blue Harley sitting on a bike lift. The scent of oil and exhaust hit my nose in the closed-in space.

Skully picked Jake up and planted him on a barstool. "So, how do you like it?" Jake's eyes were wide with wonder, looking around at the tools hanging on the wall, and the bike on the lift.

He turned back to Skully. "Are you my dad?"

"Yes, Jake. I'm your dad. Is that okay with you?"

Jake's face lit up, and he grinned. "Yeah, it's okay with me."

I felt another lump land in the pit of my stomach. I suddenly felt like an outsider, intruding on their conversation. I struggled to hold back tears.

Skully turned to me, as I just stood there, frozen. "I'm his father, Tanya."

I didn't know what to say and just wanted to flee. I handed him the bag of subs. "I brought you some lunch. I'm running late and I have to get back to the salon. You can share it with Jake, okay?"

He took the bag from me. "Please don't go. Stay and have lunch with us. You bought enough for the three of us."

The three of us.

"No, I really need to get back to work." I smiled at Jake. He was riding his two toy motorcycles down imaginary roads in front of him. "Nice meeting you, Jake. Enjoy lunch with Skully, okay?"

The motorcycles froze in mid-flight. "Nice meeting you, Miss Tanya. Thanks!"

I had no idea how old he was. Maybe he was three or four?

I cupped Skully's warm cheek and caressed the roughness of his stubbled beard. "Have lunch with Jake. Spend some time with him. I'll catch up with you later this week." I planted a quick kiss on his lips, fully aware that Jake was watching us.

I walked quickly back to my car and felt totally numb as I drove away. Owen had a son. He was a father. I couldn't hold back the tears anymore and began to sob. I made sure to wipe the mascara streaks away and blew my nose before going back into the salon to work my next appointment.

"I got the DNA test results back today. Ninety-nine percent that Jake is my son." Owen's deep voice came through my phone.

It took two weeks for the DNA results. Owen swiped the inside of Jake's mouth with a big Q-tip and did the same to himself and sent them in a large envelope to a local DNA lab. Jake looked identical to Owen, an exact miniature version of him. Owen didn't have any pictures of himself when he was a child, but I had no doubt that he had looked just like Jake.

Owen continued, "I met Jake's grandmother—Brittany's mother. Her name is Kathy. She's a nice woman. We talked when she came to the shop to pick up Jake. She seems to just want what's best for him. He's four-years-old. Kathy has him in daycare during the afternoon while she's at work. Brittany can't hold a job, and when she does have one, she barely makes minimum wage. Kathy pretty much raises and provides for him. Now that I know it's legit, I want to help and give her money to support Jake. I'm going through the right channels and child support system to get all that worked out now. "

"There is just so much for you to take on now, Owen."

"I know, and I'm fucking happy, thrilled, and terrified—all at the same time. I have no idea how to be a father. Kathy wants me to help her out. I can spend some time with him during the week. He'll be starting Kindergarten this fall."

"Who is Brittany to you? Were you in a relationship with her?" I just needed to know.

"She was a sweet butt. She hung around the Hell Hounds. We were together only a few times. That's why I needed to get the DNA test. I needed to make sure Jake was really my son."

Silence.

"You still there, Tanya?"

"Not sure what we do from here, Owen. You have a son. You need to put him first now."

"I will, and I need your help. Jake likes you. I'm going to pick him up tomorrow after work and take him out for a bite to eat. I want you to come with me and meet Kathy."

"Give me some time, Owen. Maybe we need a break. I need some time to digest all this—"

"Digest it with Jake and me. I'm scared shitless, Tanya." His voice cracked.

My heart sank. "I have to go, Owen."

"Wait, Tanya—"

I hung up on him, and the tears flowed as I sobbed, feeling the pain of knowing that I would have to step away from my relationship with Owen so he could spend more time with Jake as a father should with his son.

I cried as I sat in a chair across from Dr. Platt in her office. She leaned in, her folded arms on her desk, "You don't have to give birth to be a good mother, Tanya..."

My throat hurt, and I almost choked. Another

wave of sharp pain hit me. Menstrual cramp. I had miscarried two months before. Matthew had become distant since then. He felt so far away, and I withdrew from him too. When he looked at me, his eyes told me how he felt. It was my fault. What Dr. Platt was saying just didn't sink in.

"It's not your fault."

"Who do I blame, if not myself?"

"No one, Tanya. You can't do that to yourself."

"That's all I got, Dr. Platt. Guilt. And I deserve it." I rose from the chair and walked out of her office.

SKULLY

CHAOS KINGS
MOTORCYCLE CLUB

I hadn't seen Tanya or heard her voice for a few weeks since she hung up on me. I felt alone again but also so grateful for Jake. I went to visit him a few times and talked with Kathy and gave her money to help with anything Jake needed. Brittany would stop by Kathy's house every so often, but her visits to see Jake became less and less frequent. I passed her once as I came by Kathy's and realized that I didn't remember much about her. We hung around and fucked a few times during the days I smoked too much weed regularly. I learned from Kathy that she'd never really been around to take care of Jake. Kathy did everything and anything she could for him. And she seemed grateful that I had stepped up to help. How could I not? Knowing that Jake was my son lifted my heart, and I wouldn't have wanted it any other way. I didn't know who my parents were, and I wanted Jake to know who his father was.

I told my Chaos brothers about Jake, and they actually congratulated me with hard slaps on the back. I asked them and the women in the coven anything and everything about kids—what do they play with these days? How do you keep a four-year-old boy entertained? I didn't know a damn thing. And even though I was aching inside, missing Tanya, I had Chaos. And Jake.

Kathy was kind enough to let me borrow her car, so I could take Jake out for a sandwich at a local deli, and then to Mountain Lake County Park—the same park I rode Tanya to after leaving the CrowBar. Jake walked along beside me on the path around the small lake. The late summer heat and humidity got us both breaking out in a sweat during the short hike. He was the spitting image of me with dark hair and dark eyes, wearing khaki shorts, a tank, and his favorite chucks. I wore a tank, too, but my jeans clung to me, and my black boots felt heavy as I walked alongside him.

"I told all my buddies and Amanda that you ride a motorcycle, Dad. They all think it's really cool!" Jake said as he walked with his little hands shoved in the pockets of his shorts.

"Who's Amanda?"

"She's a friend. My buddies tell me that I shouldn't have girls as friends because they don't like the same things that us boys like. And that they smell funny."

I chuckled at that. "Well, yeah. Girls do smell, but not funny, Jake. Someday, you and your buddies won't think they smell funny. And I think it's cool you have Amanda as a friend. Friends are hard to find."

"Do you have friends, Dad?"

"I sure do. I have some excellent friends. They're like my family."

He leaned his head back to look up at me. "What are their names?"

"Well, there's Wez, Ratchet, Gunner, Magnet, Rocky, Spider. And girls too. There's Sam, Madge, Honey, Kat, and Tanya..."

God, I missed her.

"I like Tanya. I think she's really nice and pretty too." He had a sudden pink blush to his cheeks.

"Yeah. I like her too. And we're all part of a club. Do you know what a club is?'

His brows crinkled together as he looked down at his chucks. "No. What's a club?"

"A club is like a family. Your closest friends and

buddies. And even girls too. You take care of them, and they take care of you."

"Like how you, Gramma, and Mom take care of me?"

"Yeah, buddy, like that."

"Will I get to meet them someday?"

I couldn't ride Jake on my bike, but since I had Kathy's car, I thought that day would be the perfect day to do just that.

"How about today?"

I pulled in the clubhouse lot in Kathy's car. Magnet and Wez stood next to Shrek's Fat-Boy admiring the new set of ape hanger bars and a new clutch and brake cables I installed on it the week before.

Jake sat in the passenger seat, and his eyes lit up. "Wow! That's a really cool looking bike, Dad!"

"I put those high handlebars on that bike. That guy right there with the cigar in his mouth? That's his bike. We call him Shrek."

"Like Shrek from the movie *Shrek*?"

"Yep, just like the movie. Doesn't he look a bit like him?"

"Yeah, he does!" Jake giggled.

All three of them turned around and watched me park the car. We unbuckled our seat belts and climbed out, and I introduced him to my Chaos brothers. "Jake, meet Shrek, Magnet, and Wez."

He already had his little hand out and shook theirs, saying hello.

Wez shook Jake's hand last. "How ya doin', little man? You look just like your dad."

Jake's full attention was focused on Shrek's bike.

"Come over and check out the bike. Your dad put those badass handlebars on it."

Jake looked up at me as his little brows lifted. "He said *ass*, Dad."

I couldn't shield Jake from the cussing, and there was a lot of that when you were around the Chaos Kings. "Yeah. Well, only grown-ups can say that word. It wouldn't be good if you said that around your grandma or your day care buddies. Got it?

"Got it, Dad."

"Sorry about that, man," Wez mumbled.

Magnet shook Jake's hand next and picked him up, planting him on the seat of Shrek's bike. And his mouth could only form the word *Wow*.

I stepped away with Wez and lit a smoke, watching Jake as he grinned from ear to ear and nodding his head at whatever Magnet and Shrek were telling him.

"I'm a lucky motherfucker, Wez," I mumbled low so that Jake couldn't hear me cuss.

"Yeah, brother. You are. He seems like a good kid."

"I told him about the club. That I had a family. Thought this was a good time to bring him by and meet some of you. I'm really glad I did."

"Bring Jake over to the clubhouse anytime, man. It's pretty much rated PG around here during the day. And it'd be way past his bedtime when all hell breaks loose. So, how are you and my pretty girl getting along?"

I exhaled a drag. "Not sure. This whole *dad* thing scared her a bit, I can feel it."

"Just give her some time so she can let it all sink in. She had a hard breakup with that pretty boy, Matthew. I don't know much about it, but Magnet does. She may be afraid to fall hard again, giving all of yourself to someone. It's a scary thing to be vulnerable."

I dropped my smoke on the asphalt and crushed it with my boot heel. Despite his looks, Wez could get pretty deep sometimes. "Yeah. Thanks, Wez."

It felt so new to me, and it felt good to have a

friend to talk to. A brother to talk to. I knew I could get used to it.

Later that week, I sent pics to Tanya of Jake sitting on Shrek's bike. She texted back that she liked them, but nothing else. I took what Wez said as good advice and gave her time. I was scared shitless though. Scared that I would lose her. So, I kept myself busy at Hardcore Cycles and did the best I could every day for Jake. And I didn't feel as alone anymore. I had a son and my club. But Having Tanya back in my life would make me complete. A man, a lover, a brother, a father.

It was midafternoon, and I just finished installing a new light bulb on the back fender of a sporty when I turned to the sound of thundering pipes outside the bay door of the garage at Hardcore Cycles. It was Hammer and Muddy on their bikes, revving their throttles as they laughed.

Hammer let off his throttle. "Hey, Gimp! Do you really think wearing those pussy-ass Chaos colors is gonna protect you from gettin' another ass beatin'?"

I stood there, wiping my dirty hands on a rag. "You want another shot at me? I'm right here. Let's do this. Just you and me." "

They twisted their throttles and took off burning rubber off their back tires. A big hand clamped down on my shoulder. "If they come back, I'll introduce them to my Smith and Wesson." It was Torque.

"They won't come back. At least, not today." I looked down at my clenched fists then pulled out the pack of smokes from my back pocket and lit one.

TANYA

CHAOS KINGS
MOTORCYCLE CLUB

I smiled, looking at the pics of Jake on Shrek's bike. His eyes were round with excitement, giving two thumbs up to Skully as he snapped the photos from his phone. Magnet, Wez, and Shrek stood around Jake and the bike, smiles on their faces too. But I had felt only sadness and loneliness lately because I missed Owen. I missed looking at him, touching him. Hearing his voice.

I felt undeserving, that I shouldn't be around children because I had aborted one and miscarried another. It wasn't fair to wedge myself between Owen and Jake. They needed each other. They didn't need me.

I was curled up on my couch on my day off, flipping channels on the TV with the remote, when my phone rang. Skully lit up my screen.

"Hi, Skully."

"Hi, Tanya. How've you been? I miss you a ton." His deep voice made my heart skip a beat.

"I miss you too; how is Jake? Thanks for sending me those pics. He looked like the happiest boy on the planet sitting on Shrek's bike."

"Yeah. He loved it and bragged to all his buddies at day care, including his friend, Amanda."

"A girlfriend, huh? He's going to be just like his dad, having tons of girlfriends."

"I don't want to even think about that. Not just yet. I know I'll have to give him that talk about girls someday. The reason I called is to ask you out on a date with me tonight. A traveling carnival stopped into town for the weekend, and they're all set up in the parking lot by the bookstore Sam works at. Some Chaos brothers are meeting me there. I want to bring Jake with us too. I don't have a car, so I was hoping you could go pick him up from Kathy's house and bring him to the bike shop. Then we can ride together to the carnival?"

He wanted me to come with them?

I couldn't speak.

"Please, Tanya? Jake wants to see you again. And Chaos will be there too. Sounds like fun, don't it?"

"Sure. Okay, Owen. I'd like that. I'll go pick Jake up for you and bring him to the shop. Is five thirty good?"

"Hot damn! Thanks, Sweet Cheeks! I promise we'll be on our best behavior tonight."

"You shouldn't promise me that, Skully. Who knows? Maybe I don't want you on your best behavior later. When we're alone."

"Hot damn!"

I felt like a giddy teenager, going out on a date with a sexy bad boy biker. Hearing Owen's voice over the phone brightened my mood and warmed my heart. It was exhausting to mope around every day, feeling sorry for myself. Owen needed my help and to pick up Jake for him, and something switched on inside me. Maybe it was that maternal instinct that comes naturally to some women. But I had never felt it before until then.

I dressed in one of my hot pink blouses, with some jeans and flip flops, dabbing on some mascara and pink shiny lip gloss. I combed my fingers through my hair, giving it a messy, tousled look. I puckered my lips and kissed my image in the mirror and smiled at myself. I was pretty in pink.

It was five o'clock when I climbed into my car to go pick up Jake from Kathy's house.

When I buckled my seat belt, a large hand clamped over my mouth.

"Shh..." The deep male voice whispered next to my ear, as the sharp point of a blade pricked the side of my neck. "You're Skully's whore, right?" I nodded, squeezing my eyes shut. I was frozen in terror. *Was it Rusty again?*

"I'm going to take my hand off your mouth. You better just do as I tell you and don't make a fucking sound. Start the car and drive. I'll tell you where to go."

SKULLY

CHAOS KINGS
MOTORCYCLE CLUB

Hearing the sound of Tanya's voice over the phone earlier today made my heart skip a few beats. I couldn't wait to see her pull up in her car with Jake. It was about five minutes past six as I stood outside the bike shop finishing up a smoke. She was late. I pulled out my phone and called her. But her phone rang five times, then went straight to her voice mail. I squeezed the phone, rubbing the back of my neck, feeling tense and anxious.

I flicked the cigarette butt, and it arced through the air and landed in a water puddle when my phone lit up with Tanya's name. And a text message:

"Hounds got me. U want me back U no where to find me."

A tight knot formed in the pit of my stomach. I hurried to my bike and climbed on.

"You need some help, Skully?" Torque called out as he locked up the front door of the shop.

I hurried, strapping on my lid with clumsy fingers. "The Hounds got to Tanya. They're taking her to their clubhouse."

"Don't go alone. Bring your brothers with you, man!"

"I don't have time." I started the bike, stomped the shifter down to first, opened the throttle and burned rubber onto the road.

In fifteen minutes flat, I pulled into the Hell Hounds clubhouse lot. I parked next Tanya's car. Kicking the stand down, I leaped off the bike, not bothering to take my lid and shades off. I stormed through the opened doorway, full of fiery rage, my hands clenched tight, my jaw ticked, my head pounded.

I saw Tanya sitting at their bar on an old rusty stool. She didn't have a shirt on as her arms crossed over her chest, trying to cover herself in a light pink bra. She cried out, jumping off the stool, and clung to me. I wrapped my arms tight around her soft, shaking body. She sobbed against my neck.

"I got you, Tanya. I'm here." I leaned down to look at her, fearing the worst. Her eyes were red and puffy from crying, but there were no bruises. Thank god. "Did they touch you?"

She shook her head. "No, Owen. I'm okay. Where is Chaos? Did you come here alone?"

"Yeah—"

The sound of slow clapping came from behind us.

"How fucking romantic. Gets my dick hard, Skully. Really, it does," Hammer mocked. Muddy stood beside him, clapping along with him.

"These disgusting dogs want *you*, Owen," Tanya said as she shook, but the tone in her voice was steady.

"I know." I pulled my T-shirt over my head and put it over hers. "I want you to go now. Get out of here. I'll work this out."

"No!"

"Get out, whore. Unless you want to stay and watch?" Hammer grinned, his eyes roaming over Tanya's body.

"Fuck you!" she barked at Hammer and placed her hand on my cheek, her eyes lit with fire. "You're not alone, Owen, you understand? And you better get used to it. Chaos is your tribe. Your family. Jake loves you. I love you."

A feeling of calmness washed over me, and the

painful emptiness and anxiety were gone. "I love you, too, Tanya." I smashed my mouth over hers. She moaned as I held her tight against me.

"Now, go."

She hurried out, and I listened as she reached her car. The headlights came on as I heard the tires roll over the graveled asphalt, and she left. She was alive and safe.

Hammer pounded his knuckles together, cracking them as Muddy stood there chuckling.

I glared at them both and smiled. "Okay, Hammer. Let's do this."

The taste of my own blood filled my mouth. Bits of a broken molar crunched against the inside of my left cheek. My left eye was swollen shut. My whole head fucking hurt like a son of a bitch, and I felt a painful knot on the side of my skull. I sat in a wooden chair, my hands tied behind my back with an electrical cord. My hands went numb as my head hung down, my chin rested on my chest. Blood and drool splattered onto my crotch.

Hammer had started with my face and did a

good job of it. And he would get to other parts of me later.

Hammer and Muddy had led me to one of the rooms in the clubhouse, this one used exclusively to beat people to a pulp. It was empty with only one light bulb with a pull chain in the ceiling, and the wooden chair I was tied to. It smelled of piss, vomit, mold, and rotting meat.

Hammer stood in front of me, his bloody fists clenched at his sides. "You fucked your brothers over because of some cunt? Then you go and join a pussy motorcycle club?" He grabbed a fistful of my hair and wrenched my head back to look at him. "Now listen here, you fucking gimp, you're goin' to tell me what happened to that twenty-five grand!"

I hurled a glob of spit and blood right between his eyes. He let go of his grip on my hair as his head snapped back. I chuckled. "You stupid shit. I made good with Knuck. *Your* President."

"What the fuck you slobberin' about?" Hammer looked like a dumbass staring at me with spit and blood oozing down his face.

I tried to open my left eye with no luck. "That money belongs to Knuck. And I'm guessing he doesn't want to share any of it with you or your filthy dogs."

He started to pace in front of me as he clenched his fists covered in my blood. Then he leaned down and was up in my face again. "*You* made good with Knuck. But I ain't done with you yet."

He walked to the corner of the room and lifted a sledgehammer and swung it back and forth, "Got any last words, you pussy-ass-going-to-be dead motherfucker?"

I dropped my head back down. This was it, the end of me. My death. Just my luck. I was alone and lost all my life. Then Tanya found me. The Chaos Kings found me. They gave me what I needed. A home. A family. And I had a son. Jake. And I loved him. He was a part of me. He always would be, even after I was dead. And he would never be alone. He had Tanya. He had his grandmother and mother. And he had the Chaos Kings.

"Yeah." I spit more blood, and it landed on my boot. "Watch your back, Hell Hound, because Karma is one *hell* of a bitch. She'll come back around for you. And the Chaos Kings MC will be right there with her."

I squeezed my eyes shut, waiting for the swing of the sledgehammer that would smash my skull in.

"Arrggh!" Hammer roared in pain. Then there

was the sound of his body landing face down on the floor next to my boot.

My wrists were suddenly cut away, the painful feeling of pin prickly needles shooting through my hands as the blood rushed back into them. I fell forward, but my left arm was lifted and wrapped around a man's shoulders, his arm around my waist.

"I got you, brother. Let's go." Magnet lifted me off the chair. I hung on to him as he half carried me out of that room and helped me climb into the passenger side of Ratchet's truck.

"You look like shit, Skully," Ratchet grumbled as he drove me away from the Hell Hounds clubhouse. I leaned my head against the passenger window and passed out.

The softness of a pillow that smelled like Tanya cradled the back of my skull. I was in her bed. A soothing warm wet cloth was pressed lightly against the bashed-up parts of my face. I couldn't open my left eye. I opened my right eye to the sudden pain of a sharp needle. There was blonde woman I didn't recognize standing over me, her eyes focused on what she was doing with my face.

I sat up. "Where's Tanya?"

"Shh. She's here, Owen. Relax," the woman whispered.

My head landed back on the pillow. I closed my one good eye.

Darkness. Dreams. Tanya's thighs wrapped snug around my hips and the rush of air pushing us as I ride us together on the Super Glide. Jake sitting on Shrek's bike, a wide grin on his face. A spitting image of me.

TANYA

CHAOS KINGS
MOTORCYCLE CLUB

I slept with Owen in my bed that night. I placed my cheek on his chest to listen to his steady breathing. I exhaled and cried tears of relief. He was alive.

I didn't know what the Chaos Kings would find when they got to the Hounds' clubhouse earlier that night.

When I left Owen there and drove away, I pulled out my phone from my back pocket and called Magnet. I was hysterical as he told me to get to my place as soon as I could, and that he, along with Ratchet and Wez were already on their way to that clubhouse to get Owen out. That Torque had called him as Owen was heading there to save me.

Magnet half-carried Owen into my apartment, with Wez and Ratchet following close behind. He had been badly beaten, his face covered in blood.

Magnet brought him into my bedroom, and Owen collapsed on my bed. I owed everything I had to Dr. Platt. She took my phone call late that night, listening to my sobs, pleading for a huge favor. I really didn't expect her to come, but when she showed up at my apartment, I broke down in her arms. She went to work fast, cleaning Owen's wounds, and stitching up the deep cut above his left eye. Luckily, he had no other injuries to the rest of his body. She left me some painkillers to give him and a sedative to help him sleep.

Owen slept throughout the next day, as the bruises began to heal to a shade of blue and purple. He woke up a few times to find me snuggled up next to him. The side of his mouth lifted in a smile, then his brows knitted together when he felt the pain of the cut on his lip. I combed my fingers lightly through his dark, messy hair to soothe him. He moaned and fell back to sleep.

The next day, I climbed out of bed, putting on my pink robe and went to my kitchen to make some coffee. When I carried a cup back to my room, Owen was sitting up. His back leaned up against the headboard, covered only with my comforter decorated with hot pink flowers. His jeans and boxers were on the floor next to his boots. His left eye was healing and looked a little better.

"How long have I been out, Sweet Cheeks?" His deep voice was groggy.

I opened a bottle of water on the nightstand and handed it to him. "Drink, or you'll get dehydrated. You slept two days, baby."

He guzzled down the whole bottle of water and smiled, making my stomach flutter.

When he placed the empty bottle back on the nightstand, he was quick and snatched me around the waist and brought me down on top of him. I squeaked when I landed on top of his hard body as his arms wrapped around me.

His warm palm caressed my ass cheek and squeezed. "Mmm. So soft..." he whispered as he nuzzled my neck.

I gasped as his palm kneaded my ass, and I felt his hardness against my stomach. "Owen, you need to rest. We have lots of time for that later."

He leaned back to look into my eyes. "I've rested enough, baby. I need to feel you." He ground his hips against my stomach, and I could tell that he was *definitely* ready. No more thinking. No more worrying. I planted my mouth over his and our tongues collided. I moaned as he shoved the comforter down and his hard cock sprung free. He fumbled, pulling my robe up as I climbed on him and straddled his hips, impaling myself on his hard, swollen erection. His hands gripped my hips.

"That's it, baby. Ride me and take what you want," he demanded, and I did. I gyrated and ground against him, reaching between our bodies to rub my clit lightly.

"Yes, Tanya, touch yourself and come on my cock. You're so fucking beautiful." His deep husky voice sent me over that rising pinnacle, and a delicious orgasm came crashing over my body. I cried out, panting, my hips moving faster as his own breathing became rough, shaky. Then he roared as his hot cum exploded inside my warm softness. I laid over him, and he held me as we both calmed our heavy, fast breathing.

Owen moved suddenly. "Shit! I need to call Kathy—"

"I called her, Owen. Jake's okay. I didn't tell Kathy the whole story, only that you got roughed up by some bad guys who tried to rob you and that you're okay and just needing a few days to recover."

He relaxed, holding me tighter. "Thank you,

Tanya. I wouldn't be alive if it weren't for you. You saved me. You were there for me. You were there for Jake."

I smiled. "I guess I *am* your Wonder Woman, huh?"

He chuckled. "Yes, you are. And always will be."

SKULLY

CHAOS KINGS
MOTORCYCLE CLUB

I called Torque and thanked him for getting the word to Magnet and my Chaos brothers that night. I took a few more days off and stayed with Tanya at her apartment, and Magnet came over to visit. I didn't remember much about that night, and I need to know how I got out alive.

We sat in Tanya's living room as Magnet rehashed all that happened as he slouched on the couch, his arms folded over his chest. "Ratchet reached out to Knuck and told him the situation, that Hammer and Muddy had you at their clubhouse. And that we were coming to get you out. Knuck didn't even have a problem it, and he had no problem with us Chaos Kings. Ratchet didn't give a fuck about that twenty-five grand to save Sam. Knuck has way too many dipshits in his club, and they won't last long. Some other diamond club will move in someday and wipe them all out."

I had cloudy images in my head of Magnet, cutting me away from that electrical cord that cut the circulation off to my hands. And that he called me brother. "I remember Hammer landing flat on his face. And you getting me out of there. How did *that* happen?'

Magnet doubled over and began to laugh that ended with a cackle. "I can't take any credit for that. That was all Wez, brother. He came through that door first, and not a second too late, cause you would have been a dead man. Hammer was getting ready to bash your head in with a sledgehammer. But Wez struck that motherfucker with his cattle prod."

"A cattle prod?"

"Yeah. Wez likes to use his good ol' cattle prod when he needs to get out of a sticky situation. He zapped Hammer in the back a few times, then right between his ass cheeks and his balls. Motherfucker went down like a ton of bricks!" He chuckled again.

"Cattle prod?" The image of Hammer lying face down by my feet just became a lot more entertaining for me.

"I thought you would've figured Wez out by

now. He's into kink, and he's got some fetishes, plus he's a sadist."

"I guess you just never really know a person sometimes, huh?" My impression of Wez was a tad different now.

"So, I got you to Ratchet's truck, rode your bike out of there, and Wez followed me on his. We brought you here to Tanya's."

Magnet stood from the couch and huffed, rolling his eyes. "I gotta meet up with Becky and Brandy. They want me to take them to see a movie. I'd rather go film our own movie in my bedroom."

"What movie are you going to see?" Tanya asked.

"I don't know and don't care, sis. I'll just sit and wait to see how long the girls stay interested in the movie," he pointed down to his crotch, "before they steer their attention to all *this* I got for them."

Tanya rolled her eyes. "Ugh. Just keep it in your pants, Magnet."

"I can't make any promises that have *anything* to do with what's in my pants." He nodded toward the duffle bag he dropped on the couch next to me, "I brought some of your things over from the clubhouse, brother."

"Thanks, Magnet."

He planted a kiss on Tanya's forehead and left for his movie date.

Tanya moved and planted her soft little ass on my lap. "I thought maybe you'd like to live here with me, so I asked Magnet to bring over some of your things from the clubhouse." Her voice was soft, almost a whisper.

I reached up to touch her warm cheek. "You thought right, Sweet Cheeks.

TANYA

CHAOS KINGS
MOTORCYCLE CLUB

I waited for Owen while sipping on my coffee in the kitchen and watching some local news on the TV. He'd been standing in front of the mirror for a while and wouldn't come out of the bedroom. I walked in to see him as he shrugged his shoulders, raking his hand through his hair. He stood one way and then turned the other way. I moved to stand behind him and combed both my hands through his dark, messy hair. "All the other kids' mothers at the school are going to be checking out my hot-as-fuck ol' man today."

"Yeah, and so is Jake's kindergarten teacher. And not in a *good* way. I'm not so sure now that this was a good idea. Maybe Kathy should take Jake instead of me." He grumbled, looking so sexy to me as I looked at his reflection in the mirror.

It was parent-teacher night, and Jake was going to start kindergarten the following week. He was so excited to make new friends and meet his teacher. Owen was living with me in our one-bedroom apartment. We had Jake over to stay some nights during the week and worked out a good schedule with both Kathy and Brittany so we all could share time with him.

I wrapped my arms around him and looked into his eyes through the mirror's reflection. "You're Jake's father. And Kathy wants you to go with him and so does he. You will do just fine. Plus, it's good to meet Jake's teacher."

He covered my arms with his. "Yeah, you're right. I want to be part of his life, and I want him to know who his father is. I don't know if I'm going to be good at this parenting thing, but I'll figure it out as I go along."

"*We* will figure it out together, Owen." He showed me that warm, handsome smile of his that still made my stomach do somersaults.

We planned to sign a new lease and move us into a two-bedroom apartment in a few months so Jake could have his own bedroom. And we would decorate it with his most favorite thing—motorcycles.

THE END

Continue the CHAOS KINGS MOTORCYCLE CLUB with book 3, *Coveted by CHAOS,*

Available now!

ALSO BY LINNY

Sin City Fets

Switched

Capitol Corruption Series

Pushed

CKMC

Salvation in Chaos

Deep in Chaos

Coveted by Chaos

Claimed in Chaos

Torque (Novella)

Berzerkers MC

Struck in the Crossfire

Anthologies

Twisted Tales of Mayhem: 2019 MMM Special Edition

Dominated by Desire: A BDSM Anthology

Novella

Neon Summer: A Novella

Crossing the Line

ABOUT LINNY

Linny grew up in Northern Virginia, right outside Washington DC. She's both a book worm and biker chick and now an indie romance writer. Her debut novel, "Salvation in Chaos" was released in January of 2018. She loves to write MC Romance, Mobster Romance and Erotica.

If you do like her, (and I really hope you do!) you can follow her anywhere and everywhere.

Website: https://linnylawless.com

Newsletter Sign Up: https://mailchi.mp/772f49e20225/linnylawlessnewsletter

Facebook page: https://www.facebook.com/Linnylawlessromance

Chaos Coven Clubhouse: http://bit.ly/2DZQuHR

Instagram: https://www.instagram.com/linnylawless

Goodreads: https://www.goodreads.com/user/show/73729078-linny-lawless

BookBub: https://www.bookbub.com/authors/linny-lawless

Twitter: https://twitter.com/LawlessLinny

Amazon Page: https://www.amazon.com/Linny-Lawless/e/B078GYZ86K

59986425R00113

Made in the USA
Middletown, DE
13 August 2019